A STATEN ISLAND LOVE LETTER 4:

THE FORGOTTEN BOROUGH

JAHQUEL J.

D1563543

TEXT UCP TO 22828 TO SUBSCRIBE TO OUR MAILING LIST

If you would like to join our team, submit the first 3-4 chapters of your completed manuscript to Submissions@UrbanChapterspublications.com

A NOTE FROM THE AUTHOR:

I said part three was the finale, but I realized it is unfair for me to introduce you to characters and then cut their story short. For those who have left reviews telling me that I should have ended it, this isn't for you. This is for all my readers who want more, and I must admit, I give them what they want. I think that's why I've been able to stay in this industry for five years. I listen to my audience and they have told me they wanted a part four. Well, I'm about to give you guys what you want. I pray it's everything that you've been wanting, plus more.

This book focuses on all the couples. They all face a new challenge from issues that they have to handle. You may wonder why you hear from one couple more than another. Trust, this book has been planned and I have a method to my madness. *Inserts evil laugh*

Some things may happen that you won't like, but we all have read a book or watched a movie that ended a way we didn't like. You'll live.

I don't write fairytales, so if that's what you're expecting, respectfully bow out. Things get deep, but so does real life.

This series means a lot to me. I don't know if I shared this with you guys, but I was writing this book and I had everything planned but the beginning. My husband happened to be cooking dinner and listening to music on our television. He had on YouTube while he cut up onions. I sat on the couch with my laptop in my notebook, completely perplexed. I didn't know how I wanted to start this book. The video for *Double Up* by Nipsey Hussle came on the TV, and I was wrapped up in it from beginning to end.

When the video ended, I downloaded his album and was writing my ass off. My husband has always been a big Nipsey Hussle fan. It was that video that gave me the inspiration to pen A Staten Island Love Letter.

R.I.P Nipsey Hussle

The Marathon Continues, Beloved.

Make sure to join and follow me on all my social media to stay in loop of all things me!

PLAYLIST FOR A STATEN ISLAND LOVE LETTER 4

Click here for the playlist —> https://apple.co/30Oux8q

Never Ever – Ciara4am – Nipsey Hussle

Higher – Nipsey Hussle
Stubborn Ass– Young M.A
That's why – Eric Bellinger ft Nipsey Hussle
Girls Like You – Miguel
Great one – Jessie Reyez
Hate it or love it – Nipsey Hussle
Homebody Remix – Lil Durk ft Teyanna Taylor
Karma Krys – Young M.A
Big Ole Freak – Megan thee stallion
Cheers to you – Playa
Talk – Khalid
Double Up – Nipsey Hussle
My place – Nelly ft Jahiem
This I promise to you – NSYNC
Make it work – Neyo

Do you – Neyo
NWA – Miguel
Coffee remix – Miguel
You Stay – Meek Mill
I Care – Beyoncé

SYNOPSIS:

Ghost and the crew are back with a whole new world of issues. While the streets are calm, their home lives are far from that. Free is carrying their son and Ghost is over the moon with the pregnancy. This is his second chance to parent and become one with Free. While they're preparing for the birth of their son, a curveball comes out of thin air and rocks the foundation of their home. How will Free and Ghost get through this? Just when they've find a solution and solace to their first problem, Ghost is hit with something that has the ability to take him away from Free and his children. How will Free be able to handle a new baby and this new issue? Will she stand tall and be everything that her man needs her to be? Or will she flee again like she did all those years ago?

Liberty and Staten are together and far from happy. Chanel may have accepted that she and Staten may never be together, but she's not willing to go away, especially with her about to have his first child. While Staten is trying to juggle being the head of the streets, a new dad, and a boyfriend to Liberty, will Liberty find her comfort in something else? When Liberty starts becoming distant, and Maliah and he start spending more time together, what will happen? All Staten wants is someone to love him, but with Liberty fighting her own demons, will she lose Staten's heart forever? Will Maliah fill the void that is inside Staten's heart? Or will Staten fight hard to get the woman that he loves back?

Justice and Priest are happy and welcoming their first child together. While Justice is trying to keep calm and stop freaking out over her pregnancy, Priest is battling his issues with his nieces. Love is now sixteen and has found her way into the same hoods that Kiss once frequented. While trying to raise both his nieces, keep Kiss on the right track, and raise his nephew, will he start to lose it? Especially when someone enters his life and starts to wreak havoc for both he and his family.

The crew is back and ready to give you a glimpse of their new lives. Make sure you're ready to cross the Verrazano bridge and pay that toll so that you're welcomed back into the forgotten borough; Staten Island

1

Liberty
He did 'yo ass wrong, plus your dad gone, I wanna see you happy –
Nipsey Hussle

"It's been so damn long since I've been able to hang and chill with you," Justice made sure to remind me as she rubbed her stomach.

I laughed because I knew it had been a while since me and my sisters kicked it. With both of them pregnant, the last thing I wanted to do was be around either of them. With their hormones and attitudes, I didn't want to be a target for their frustrations. Since I was off from work today, I decided to stop by and see my sister. Justice had been so busy with opening her center and being pregnant that I'm surprised she realized how long it had been since we were able to hang out.

"I've been working and trying to spend as much time with Chance as I can. With him being older, I feel like I need to visit him more," I explained and accepted the drink she offered me.

"Yeah, I understand that. Mama goes up there every week-end. I'm surprised she and auntie get along with her going to visit so much."

"They don't. Mommy takes Chance out or he stays with her in her hotel room, then they spend the weekend together," I explained.

My mother and aunt would never have a relationship and I realized that before my mother knew about Chance. My mother couldn't forgive my aunt for the way she treated Mylah, and now she was pissed with both me and my aunt for hiding Chance for her. So, instead of them building a relationship, it was now more strained than ever.

"It sucks that they can't get along for the sake of Chance," Justice sighed.

"I'm not stressing them. All I'm concerned with is spending time with my son. If both of them old hoes can't get it together, then I don't know what to tell them." I rolled my eyes and took a sip of the water Justice had given me.

"And is mommy still not talking to you?"

The way I screwed my face up told her the answer she was looking for. My mother was upset with me and refused to talk to me. She didn't even want to hear my reasonings on why I chose to keep Chance a secret. I had come to learn that my mother wasn't mad at the fact that I had a child, she was upset that I chose to trust my aunt with that secret more than her. Truthfully, I wasn't pressed to sit down and make things right with my mother either. She and my aunt had their reason for not dealing with each other and I understood that, but I wasn't about to be dragged into their beef. Especially when I had nothing to do with it. My worry was on my son and his wellbe-ing, not two grown women who have been bickering for the last twenty odd years.

"Before you go trying to tell me to make it right, I'm not doing that," I sniffled and wiped my nose.

"Sick?" Justice asked as she covered my mouth. "I can't afford to get sick and you've been sniffling since you walked through that door."

"N.. yeah," I replied and walked into the kitchen to grab some tissues. Justice's dramatic ass grabbed a face mask off the coffee table and put it over her face. "Justice, is that necessary?"

"Um, yeah. I'm going to have a healthy baby without any complications. Priest went and got all of this because the girls are always complaining about not feeling well," she added.

"Anyway," I rolled my eyes. "How is everything with baby girl?" I asked as I made my way back to the couch.

A big smile came across her face. I loved seeing my sister so happy and in love. Especially with a man that loved her just as much as she loved him. In the past, Justice had loved her ex more than she loved herself at times. It was a nice change to see her loving someone and them reciprocating those same feelings back to her. As if he wasn't surrounded by enough estrogen, he and Justice were having a baby girl. I laughed so hard when she told me that she was having a girl. Priest was walking around telling anyone who would listen that he and Justice were having a son. At first, they thought it was a boy. Then, they went to the next visit and it turned out that she was carrying a precious baby girl. With all these babies around me, I had no need to get pregnant ever again. I had Somali, Samaj, and Rain who kept me on my toes, then Free and Justice were both pregnant at the same time.

Not to mention, Chanel was due to have Staten's baby any day now. I was so happy when she went on maternity leave. Even though we semi patched things up, I knew Chanel wasn't happy about Staten choosing to be with me. She made it clear with her snide remarks when he wasn't around. Not to mention, she loved to use that damn baby to get him to come over to her place, or for her to interrupt our lives. She would use her key to Staten's house and just waddle in without using the damn door bell. I complained to Staten a few times and he liked to act like it wasn't a big deal. To me, it was a big deal. Why did this bitch have a key to your home, and I didn't have one? It was small things about Staten that pissed me off when it came to Chanel. He treated me like I was fragile and couldn't handle anything. Instead of talking to me and being real, he liked to hide

things and act like I couldn't process shit, or it would cause me to go back to using drugs.

"Why are you zoned out like that?" Justice brought me back to our conversation. "I've been talking for five minutes and you haven't blinked once," she giggled. "You okay?"

This was the part I hated the most. Everyone asking me if I was alright. I was fine. I just wanted my own space and time to think, did that mean something was wrong with me?

"I'm good. Just tired from working."

"How are you and Staten?"

I shrugged my shoulders. Depending on which one of us you asked, you would get a different answer. He would say everything was fine and we couldn't be better. If you asked me, you would get a shrug of the shoulders and a half ass answer. I guess we were fine.

"Good. I'm just trying to get a handle on this girlfriend thing. You know I haven't been in a relationship in forever."

"Take it one day at a time. You don't need to be the perfect girlfriend right away." She advised. "You need to be worried about yourself and sobriety anyway."

I hated when they brought that up. Taking care of myself was first on my list, but that didn't help me with trying to be the best girlfriend that I could be. It was hard trying to be a good girlfriend when I barely wanted to be around my boyfriend. Being around Staten just reminded me of a part of my life where I wasn't in control of myself. He made me feel like I couldn't do anything for myself. The moment he made me ask my doctor if it was good to take Tylenol was when I realized that he didn't see me as the sexy Liberty that he had waited his whole entire life to be with. He saw me as the recovering drug addict.

"I am."

"What's wrong? I feel like you're not telling me something?" Justice continued to pry. She always knew when something was off with me.

"I'm fine. Just trying to think about what I'm cooking tonight," I lied. Food was the last thing on my mind at this moment.

"Oh okay. Priest wants Kiss to move out of the house," she decided to switch the subject after staring at me for a bit.

"Really? She better not be pregnant again."

"No, she doesn't listen to her curfew and she leaves me with her baby all the damn time. I love Zamari, but I don't want to always spend my Fridays in the house watching her son while she's partying."

"Shouldn't she be in college or something? Partying should be the last thing on her mind right now."

"Yeah, she got accepted into NYU, but hasn't gone and had her admissions meeting. Her first semester check is still sitting in Priest's dresser draw. We've worked so hard on her college applications and it's like she doesn't even want to go."

"College isn't for everybody, Justice. Who says she has to go to college?" I had to be honest for a second. Kiss should have been doing something with her life, but it didn't mean that she had to go to college. It also didn't mean that she could sit around on her ass while her uncle paid for everything. The girl needed to get her a damn job or something.

"Yeah, but it needs to be for her. Hanging out in the streets isn't going to help her out." Justice damn near jumped down my

throat. I could tell she cared so much for Priest's niece from
how passionate she was about Kiss finishing school. "She has a
son and need to get a career. Even Reese wants her to go to
college."

"If she doesn't want to go then you all need to stop pushing
and pressuring her into going. Suggest a trade school or a job.
Priest owns a bunch of businesses and she can work for him."

"He really wants her to go to college. You don't understand
how bad he wants this for her," Justice tried to convince me.

"He wants her to go because he never got to finish. Priest
can't put his shit onto her. Kiss is capable of telling you guys
what she wants, but neither of you will listen. Remove yourself
as the adult and put yourself in her shoes. At eighteen, I had no
clue what I wanted to do and didn't care to figure it out either."

"Well, you weren't eighteen with a damn baby. She has a
son that she needs to provide for and can't fool around. It
doesn't matter that you raised Chance or not, but after you had
him you grinded like hell through nursing school. Kiss needs to
do the same with college."

"Whatever. This is giving me a headache and it's not even
my issue," I gave up on the conversation about Kiss.

That girl was going to run and be wild and didn't give a
damn that she had a child. Priest thought that by enrolling her
in therapy and making her finish high school that things would
go back to normal. Kiss had got a taste of being free and wild
and she didn't want to go back to that school girl that he
wanted. She was now a mother and a legal adult. Did he really
think that she would abide by curfews and enroll in college like
the good girl he had raised? She had been fucked by a hood
nigga, had a baby by him and then watched him be murdered
right in front of her while carrying his child. Kiss was no longer
the seven-year-old that adored everything her uncle did. She
was now a grown woman and was going to challenge things.

"I'm just so overwhelmed with the center and trying to keep

the girls on the right path. Love has this little boyfriend, so I've been trying to make sure she doesn't end up following after Kiss."

"I get that you and Priest are together and stuff, but that's not your job. You should be focused on your baby and business, period. Love and Kiki aren't your responsibility, Justice."

"They are. When I decided to be a part of their life that's when they became my responsibility. I can't just ignore and allow them to fuck their life up because I'm expecting my own baby."

This whole visit and conversation was pointless. I came over to kick it with my sister and now she was sitting here with tears in her eyes crying over her boyfriend's nieces. "I'm going home. You're too emotional. Between you and Freedom, I don't know who is worse." I grabbed my purse and walked over to kiss and rub her stomach.

Justice sniffled and wiped her eyes. "I'm sorry. All these emotions are everywhere, and I can't control them," she apologized and then giggled. Her stomach jiggled while she laughed.

"You're fine. I don't want to argue, and I know you can go back and forth all day. I have a few errands to run before heading home."

"Drive safe. I'm sorry that our talk got weird."

"You're fine. I needed a little distraction from everything." I laughed and headed out the door. When I was heading out, Priest was coming in with the girls from dance class.

"What's good, Lib?"

"Ain't shit. Your emotional ass woman is driving me nuts."

He laughed. "Yo, she started crying during *Toy Story 3*. Her hormones is everywhere."

My eyes watered. "Was it the part when they were going to get burned up in the fire?" He shook his head and walked past me. "What?"

"Not you too. Man, I can't with you two."

"Free cries too," I added and headed to my truck. "Go and love your woman before she break out in tears again."

"I got you," he nodded and headed into the house.

I climbed into my truck and sat down in the driver's seat for a second before I went into the glove compartment and grabbed the little baggy of white powder. I took a pinch out and lined it perfectly on my index finger and sniffed the line off my finger. Pinching the bridge of my nose, I leaned back in the chair for a second and then placed the coke back into the glove compartment. I checked myself in the mirror to make sure I didn't have any white residue on my nose before I pulled off from the curb. Did I plan on going back to the same drug that damn near ruined my life? No. I had every plan on staying clean and making sure I applied everything I learned in rehab to my everyday life. All of that worked for a month or two, then I hit a road block. The reason I was so good at my job was because I was high. When I was high, the time floated by and it didn't feel like I was working hard. It was like a slap from reality when I worked a double sober. By the end of my shift I felt like I was dying a slow and painful death. Dealing with life sober was hard as fuck.

Each time I was presented a new challenge that I didn't want to face. I would drown the issues out by getting high, but this time I couldn't do it. All the things I had to face, I had to face them sober and I couldn't do it. I tried so hard for a while and then gave in. At first, I tried to put myself on a limit. I would only do it when I got home from work. Then, I decided I would do it every other day. Eventually, I started using it as much as I could. Instead of keeping the stash in the house, I left it inside of my car. Staten thought I didn't know that he liked to do a sweep around my apartment when I was at work or sleep. It was shit like that, that made me stay away from him. Even when I was sober, he acted like I was getting high on the low when I wasn't. The one thing I promised myself was that I would continue with therapy and I wouldn't allow it to take over my life like before.

Staten's number popped up on my car's screen and I laughed. It was like he had a radar or something and would pop up or call when I was thinking about him. I pressed the green phone icon and continued to drive to the supermarket.

"Hey."

"Why you sound so dry?"

"No reason. What's up?"

"I miss you."

"I miss you too. What you doing?"

"Just came from looking at some property in Jersey."

"Oh yeah? What part?"

"Newark. There's money to be made here," he replied, and I took a deep gulp. "The fuck did you swallow, a cat?"

I let out a nervous laugh. "I was drinking some water. W... why Jersey?"

"I've been hearing about the real estate here... might need to get in on this," he spoke in code.

"Nice."

"When am I going to see you? Don't say that work shit either, I saw your schedule on the fridge too." he made sure to mention.

"I'm going to grab some food, so you can come over whenever you're done looking at properties."

"Word? You cooking?"

"Now you know nobody cooks after food shopping," I busted out laughing. Once I started, I couldn't stop laughing.

"Damn, Lib, that shit wasn't even that funny."

"Sorry," I snorted. "If you want to grab some food on your way over you can."

"Ight," he hesitantly replied.

"See you soon." I quickly ended the call. "Damn, bitch. Get your shit together," I told myself and continued to head to the supermarket.

Instead of copping in New York, I paid the toll and headed into Jersey. It was almost too easy going into Newark, finding a dealer, and getting some coke. It wasn't some of the best, but it got the job done after a few sniffs. If Staten started doing business in Jersey then that meant I would have to find somewhere else to cop my work, and I didn't have time for all of that. This should have been a sign to check myself back into rehab and get clean again, but my dumb ass saw it as a challenge. Long as I was keeping up with work, doing my job as a mother and keeping up this sober facade with Staten, I was going to be fine.

Freedom

"I JUST HATE GOING to the doctors," I admitted as Ghost helped me climb into my truck. He grabbed hold of my face and kissed me before he closed the door and walked around the truck.

"Ma, you're just nervous about the doctor calling us into his office to talk. Stop worrying yourself. I already said my prayers and I know everything will be fine," he tried to calm me down. His cool demeanor was something that brought some calm to the chaos that was currently swirling around my mind, but this time it wasn't enough for me.

"Gyson, our last appointment he took his sonogram pictures, now he's calling me in a week later to discuss something important. How are you not scared?" I rubbed my stomach and looked on as he pulled out of our iron gates.

I could tell he wasn't listening to anything I was saying as he messed with the screen to find what he wanted to listen to. At our last sonogram, the doctor said he wanted to take a closer look at the scans. I didn't think anything of it and thought it was normal. When he called last night and demanded that we come to his office first thing in the morning, my nerves were a wreck. I thought my heart was going to burst throughout the night. Meanwhile, Gyson slept like a baby and went on about his morning normally. I was terrified because I knew what it was like to have complications during pregnancy. I had only one complication when I was pregnant with the twins and that was because I was working too much. Once I was on bedrest for a few weeks, I was back to normal and delivered them at thirty-nine weeks, which was good for a pregnancy with multiples. I asked the doctor to confirm a bunch of times and I was in fact carrying only one baby this time, still I was a nervous wreck.

"Freedom, you really need to chill before you get yourself worked up. Let's just ride to the office and see what he wants to discuss before jumping to conclusions," he advised.

"Fine," I folded my arms and turned my attention out of the window.

Things between me and Gyson have been going amazing. Since we moved out of his old place and into our new home, we have been on the same page. It was like everything we went through hadn't happened at all. The twins and Rain were doing good in school and we were all just waiting for our son to be born. My mother was happy that I didn't decide to move back to Georgia. I knew she would be sad because we'd just come back and then we were trying to leave again. Now that I was pregnant, she was over my house more than me. I appreciated her because she helped me and G with the kids. The help was well needed because these days all I did was sit in the bed and snack on whatever food someone brought me. I barely left the house and did all my consultation calls from the comfort of my bed. Carrying this belly around was no joke and it took a lot out of me.

My doctor had prescribed me an inhaler because I could barely catch my breath when I walked around. Our new office was going to be in Hoboken, New Jersey. I had closed on the property last month and had been waiting to go and get my hands on the designs I had been choosing. I wasn't in a rush to get the office up and running because my main focus was my family. Gyson supported everything that I was doing and tried to step in to help whenever he could, still I was more focused on making sure my family was well taken care of. Plus, I didn't want anyone doing anything without me. And, as of right now, I couldn't even tie my shoe without losing my breath, so trying to renovate our new office would be an nightmare.

"When do you want to start my boy's nursery?" Ghost decided to switch the subject. I rolled my eyes because I knew what he was doing. He was trying to get my mind off worrying and it wasn't going to work.

"I don't know," I replied being short.

"Word? So if I hire someone to come through and do the job you wouldn't be mad?" he asked.

If looks could kill, his ass would have been dead behind that wheel. "You think I would allow someone else to do my son's bedroom? Every room in that house I've done with my team, his room won't be an exception," I spat and turned my attention back out the window.

Out the corner of my eye I saw him laughing. "You really need to chill." He exited off the highway and put his hand on my thigh.

"How are you so calm?"

"When you're used to fucked up shit happening you learn to focus on the positive. God wouldn't give me too much to handle."

"I agree, but still."

"Freedom, whatever is thrown at us I know that it will be handled. We'll handle it together, you hear me?"

"Okay." I finally agreed and decided not to continue to press the issue. "Did you hear about this little boy Somali has a crush on?" I decided to switch gears.

"I'll bust his ass," he blurted.

"She's going to have crushes. You can't beat every boy that comes along and into her life."

"Who the fuck says?"

"And what if Samaj has a crush on a girl?"

"I'd tell him to handle his thing." He laughed and I shook my head. "It's different. I don't want my girls to be out there fucking with niggas. They my princesses."

"Samaj and Samoor are different than Rain and Somali. I'm raising my girls to focus on school and shit, not boys."

"And just fuck Samaj and Samoor," I snapped. "What about their school?"

"Chill, Free. I don't want my boys involved in the game. They gonna go to college too, but I want my girls concerned with school and not no nigga."

The moment I found out that I was having a boy, I already knew what I wanted to name him. Samoor Storm Davis was the name that I had come up with. I dreamed about it, said it randomly throughout the day and made sure that Ghost was on board. When I told him the name he was excited about it. Samoor didn't know how excited we were for him to be born. Our entire house revolved around him and he wasn't even here to soak up all the attention. Ghost backed into the expecting mother's parking spot and hopped out to help me out of the truck. When my feet were planted on the ground, he took hold of my stomach and his expression grew serious. I watched as he rubbed my stomach and stared down into my eyes.

"Whatever the doctor tells us in there, just know that we're a team and we will get through anything. The past few years have been crazy, and we got through that, so I know we can get through anything."

"Okay. I love you." I reached up and caressed his face.

"I love you too." He grabbed my hand and we walked into the doctor's office. I checked in at the front and took a seat beside Ghost.

He grabbed my hand and started to rub it. "You heard from your sisters?"

"I know Justice has been trying to get her house together for the baby. With Zamari's baby stuff and Kiss being home, there isn't any room. Kiss has moved Zamari into her old room, so she doesn't have room for a nursery."

"It's about time for Kiss to get her ass out the crib. She's eighteen and old enough to get her own place. This is her first seed; she needs the space."

"I told her that. Justice doesn't want to overstep in their whole relationship, so she remains quiet."

"Shit, she need me to say something? Who the fuck told Kiss to move her shit into that room?"

"No, let them handle it," I told him.

"I'm just saying. Let Kiss come live with us, we got enough room. I bet her ass would be working and not out partying with Reese's ass."

"Reese isn't the issue. They break up every week because he finds out she was out in the club instead of home with the baby. It's Kiss and her sucky ass parenting."

"She don't even need to be having a man. Shorty should be focused on school or a job. Priest owns too much shit for her not to have a job somewhere."

"It's not our business. I try to just listen and not get involved with their stuff. Kiss knows what she's doing and likes to use the death of Zoe to play with Priest's heart strings. I get she's mourning but come on now."

"Mourning while shaking her ass at the club. This is why my girls are gonna be focused on school. That girl was raised and handed everything she wanted. She never had to worry about her next meal or where she was going to sleep. Priest raised that girl right and all she handed him was a damn baby with his enemy and excuses."

I could tell the situation was pissing him off from the vein that was bulging out the side of his neck. It always appeared whenever he was upset about something. "I understand, but we have to remember that Priest has control over his household. As much as I love Justice and wish she didn't have to deal with that shit pregnant, I have to realize that she's grown and can handle herself."

"Yeah," was all he responded with as he continued to rub my hands.

"Mr. and Mrs. Davis," my doctor came out and waved us to the back. Every time we came she called me by Ghost's last name. I constantly corrected her and told her that we weren't married, yet she still continued to call me Mrs. Davis.

It felt nice to be called Davis. We had filed the papers to change the twin's last name from McGurry to Davis and it felt nice to share the same last name with them again, even if it was only during my doctor appointments.

"Take a seat here and I'll go grab some refreshments," she said as she pointed into her office and then disappeared down the hall.

My leg shook as I fumbled with my hands. What was this woman about to tell us? It wasn't like I could read her face. She should have played Poker for a living because I couldn't read anything from her blank expression. She sat down two bottles of water and then made her way around her desk and sat down. I watched as she adjusted the expensive watch on her wrist, then typed her password into her iPad to look over our files before speaking to us about it.

"I called you both back in here to discuss something I've found on the ultrasound the last time you both were here. I didn't want to burden you both with worry until I was sure about everything. I've also spoken to three colleagues who confirmed what I already knew," she started.

"Oh God, what is it?" I gasped and Ghost grabbed my hand and held it tightly. My chest felt like it was about to explode.

"Yeah, Doc, what's going on with our baby?"

She sighed, "Your baby has a heart defect called Ebstein's anomaly. It's a rare heart defect that only affects about one in ten thousand babies."

"What is it? Can it be cured?" Ghost took the words out of my mouth and asked. I had a bunch of questions I wanted to ask, but my mouth wouldn't move to ask them.

"Ebstein's anomaly is a rare heart defect that affects the tricuspid valve. Ebstein's anomaly has a wide range of severity. And no, there's no cure for it," she explained. She reached over to her marble table and showed us an example of the defect versus a regular pumping heart."

"My baby is supposed to live with this for the rest of his life?"

"Unfortunately. My colleague is the top cardiologist at a hospital in Boston that has treated six babies with this condition. He still monitors these babies and has performed surgery on them when it was needed. With surgery and treatment, your son can be alright. It's a good thing that I caught it now instead of when he was born. We know what we're up against and we can prepare for you to give birth in the next two months."

Tears were pouring down my face as I looked at this doctor tell me to prepare for my birth. How was I supposed to do that? My damn unborn baby had a heart problem that couldn't be cured. Imagine being a parent and finding out that your child had an issue you couldn't fix? My baby was supposed to be perfect.

"How do you expect us to prepare for birth? Is it something that we did to cause this or something?" I held onto Ghost's arm as he asked all the right questions.

"There is nothing that either of you did. Like I said, this is a rare defect and there was no way for either of us to know that this would happen. I do have a recommendation, but it's totally up to the both of you."

"What is it?" I choked out.

"My colleague wants to treat your baby. When you're close to delivering, he wants to have you come give birth in Boston where he can be there to take the baby right into surgery soon as he comes into this world. Obviously, you'll be having a C-section. I know how much you wanted to try and push, but this is the safest way to deliver the baby."

"Fuck all that pushing shit. Is he the truth?"

"He's the best. I use him and another colleague who is based in London when I have issues like this with my patients. I wouldn't recommend going overseas since they do things different from the states, but my colleague in Boston is my top recommendation. He also works with a great OB/GYN who has no issues stepping in to deliver the baby."

"No, I want...Need you," I told her.

"I can see if I can get privilege to practice there during your delivery. I don't see it being an issue with the nature of this case." She jotted something down in her notepad. "I want you both to know that we will do everything in our power to make sure that this baby has the best fighting chance as possible."

Ghost reached his hand across her desk and shook her hand. "I'll get to finding us a spot in Boston."

"Mr. Davis, you don't need to go right away. I would say once she hits eight months, you both should make your way to Boston so you can meet the team and everyone."

"Nah, if I need to go now, then that's what's going to be done," he told her and stood up. I tried to wipe my tears, but the more I tried to stop them, the more they kept coming.

"Freedom, we're going to fight this. You have the best working for you. Call me if you have any questions, you have my personal number," she told me as Ghost carefully pulled me out of the office. "I also want to do weekly sonograms to make sure the condition doesn't worsen," she poked her head out of the door.

"I'll schedule one for her at the front," he told her.

I stood there while he scheduled us another appointment and then we made our way out of the office. Sniffling, I tried to stop the damn tears and be strong for my baby, but I couldn't. The truth was that I wasn't strong enough for this. Ghost gently pushed me against the truck and took my face into his hands.

"This shit is hard and I'm not gonna front it got me fucked up. Having something wrong with my kids drives me crazy and makes me want to fuck everything up, but you have to be strong and not stress him out. You stressing means that he's feeling that shit and it's not good on his heart. It's hard ma, and if I could take this away from him, I would, but I can't, and you can't either. Stop this crying because we got the best working for us, ight?"

I sniffled and nodded my head as the last tears fell down my cheeks. "Okay. You're right," I agreed.

I felt like just when things were going good for us, something hit us out of the left field. All I wanted was to prepare for the birth of our son and create memories that we never got to experience together. I had to stop being so emotional and put on a brave front for my kids and unborn son.

"Mama, why can't I get my nails done with real nails?" Rain came and climbed up in the bed beside me.

I stood going over a final design and turned my attention to her. "Baby girl, you're too young and your daddy is too crazy," I giggled. "Stay my little angel forever, okay?"

"Okay," she sulked.

"Grab the remote and let's watch a movie on Hulu," I tried to cheer her up. In our new neighborhood, Somali had friends who came to get her, and they would spend time being little girls. I didn't mind since I had met all the parents at our first HOA meeting. Samaj was in the game room with a few of the boys he hung out with and Ghost was out back on a business call. I knew Rain was bored and I felt bad because we had no one for her to play with. There were plenty of kids her age, I just didn't want to sit in someone's house while she had her playdate. I knew I shouldn't have been so antisocial, but with everything going on with the baby, I just needed to sit in my own home and calm down.

"I guess..." she rolled down onto the floor and went to get the controller off the TV stand. "What movie should we watch?"

"You know what? Let's take a drive to see Auntie Justice," I suggested and closed my laptop. While I knew I should have been getting this work done so my assistant could send it to the clients, I was more concerned about Rain feeling alone.

It was already hard enough with her losing her sister, now that Summer was gone Rain didn't have anyone. Somali played with her when she could, but she was getting older and had friends. Samaj would bring her with his friends to ride bikes in the street, but I didn't force him to bring her each time he decided to leave to hang with them. There was hardly anyone that she could play with and I felt bad. It made me miss Summer that much more.

"Yay!" she cheered up and sat the remote control back down onto the table. "Need help, mama?" she asked as she came over to my side of the bed to help me climb out of the bed.

"Thank you, Boo!" I bent down and kissed her on the cheeks.

Rain started calling me mama randomly. I was cooking dinner for the kids and she asked me to pass her the ketchup and added mama at the end. I didn't force her or deny her calling me mom. This girl lost both her younger sister and mother all in the same year. The only person she had left was Ghost and I knew she was craving that mother presence in her life. I'm sure when Samaj and Somali called me mom or mommy she felt left out. As long as she felt comfortable enough to call me mama, I was good with it and didn't mind it at all.

"Should we tell daddy?" she held onto my hand as I pulled a cardigan out of the closet. I was already dressed in a long Maxi dress that I liked to lounge in. It was the only thing that felt comfortable with me carrying this huge bump around.

"Yes. I think if we disappear he might be worried about us," I giggled.

"Me, you, and baby brother are his world. Samaji pooh and Somali too," she added.

"We are." I smiled as we made our way downstairs.

Just as we were coming down the last few steps, Ghost walked in from outside with his phone in his hand. "Shouldn't you be resting?"

"Yeah, well I figured me and Rain could go over and spend some time with Justice," I explained. "The twins are with their friends and Rain is bored."

"Let me drive y'all. I don't like you driving by yourself."

"Baby, I can drive myself. Let me go over there alone, please," I begged.

Since finding out about the baby's heart condition, Ghost had been super clingy. It wasn't that I minded, I just wanted to get out the house without him rushing to grab keys to take me. That was all I really wanted and the more he stood there and stared at me, the more I knew he wasn't about to let me go alone, even if I begged.

He stared at me for a bit before he blew air out of his mouth. "Bet. Call me soon as you pull into their driveway," he finally agreed.

I reached up and kissed him on the cheek and went to grab my purse. Me and Rain felt like hostages finally being freed from the castle. I knew she needed some time out the house and I needed the same thing. Since finding out about the baby's condition, I hadn't spoken to anyone about it. Whenever Ghost tried to talk about it I cut him off and told him this wasn't the time to talk about it. It was something I thought about all day and I just didn't want to speak about it out loud. This was supposed to be a joyous time for the both of us and now we were hit with this news that was going to alter our entire lives soon as our baby boy was born.

"I'm happy to get out the house, mama," Rain said as we drove on the highway to Justice's house.

I didn't have to call because I knew that she was going to be home. Justice was scared to even breathe during her pregnancy. I understood her reasonings. She had lost so many pregnancies that she didn't want to do anything to risk this one. I understood and I prayed for her every day.

"Me too, babe. We can probably pick some ice cream up on our way home," I told her, and she clapped her hands.

Rain was the strongest little girl I had witnessed. She lost both her mother and sister and every day she still found a reason to smile. Every morning her feet hit the ground, she had a smile on her face and the innocence still remained inside of her eyes. I loved that about her the most. Even as a child, I could tell her spirit as an adult was going to be so beautiful and amazing. Soon as we pulled into Justice's driveway, I pulled my phone out and dialed Ghost's number. He answered immediately.

"We just got here. I'll call you when we're leaving," I told him.

"Bet. I love you both," he said before we both ended the call.

I climbed out of my truck and got Rain out before we headed to the front door. Just as we were about to knock on the door, Kiss opened the door with a lollipop in one hand and her son in the other. She wore short shorts, a belly shirt, and her hair was pulled into a neat bun.

"Hey Freedom!" she smiled. "Justice just got up from her nap. I thought I was about to die with this boy here," she giggled and held the door wider so we could walk inside the house.

"Ayee baby!" Justice smiled and Rain ran into her arms. "How are you, Princess?"

"I'm good Auntie... how's the baby?" Rain placed her small hand over Justice's stomach. Justice was glowing with happiness and everything that Priest was pouring into her. I had never seen her like this before and it was something nice to welcome for once.

"She's getting so dang big."

"Hey Jus!" I kissed her on the cheek and made my way into the kitchen to fix me something to eat. On the ride over here, I couldn't wait to step through the door and fix me something to eat.

"Well damn, you couldn't wait before you invaded my damn fridge," she laughed and took a seat on the stool as I pulled the ingredients out to make me a sandwich.

"Girl, I was hungry as hell on the ride over. Me and Rain were bored in the house and wanted to come check on you."

"Awe, thanks guys!" she smiled. "I'm good. Just tired and I've been up with Zamari at night because he's sick."

"Rain, go ahead and look for Love and Kiki."

"Okay," Rain ran off without another word. She was just

happy to get out of the house and not be forced to watch movies with me in bed all day.

"Justice, that's not your baby. He has a mother who should be up with him, not you."

"Free, she don't be knowing what to do and always comes into my room at night for me to take him. I just don't like hearing him suffer because his mother don't know what she's doing," she tried to explain, and I wasn't hearing any of that.

"What does Priest think about it?"

She shrugged. "He be so tired that he doesn't notice. The other morning Zamari was in the bed with us and he questioned why, but I threw him off and switched the subject."

"If he knew that Kiss was tossing the baby on you every chance she got, he would be pissed with you. What's gonna happen when you have Yasmine? You gonna juggle two babies at once?" I questioned.

"Yasmine is my main priority because she's my daughter. If I can help her, then I'll help, but my baby will always be my priority, along with Kiki and Love."

"Uh huh. Have you heard from my twin lately?" I decided to switch the subject.

My sister was one of those people that could be slapped, and then end up putting ice on the person who slapped her hand. She was way too caring and allowed people to walk over and use her. I was Kiss's age before, and I knew that's exactly what she was doing when it came to Justice. Having that baby was cool when everyone was paying her attention. Now that she had Zamari, that attention slowly faded, and her friends were concerned about partying and living their own lives. Kiss was eighteen and she wanted to do the same thing too, which is where Justice came in. She wanted to be a part-time mother and that's not how it worked.

"Justice, I put Zamari down upstairs and Love is watching him. I'll be back in a few hours. Reese isn't answering his phone and he's pissing me off." She smacked her lips as she held her phone in her hand.

"Okay, please be back before your uncle gets home. You don't want to hear his mouth," she advised.

"I will," she replied and left out the door.

All I did was shake my head because this was crazy. According to Kiss, she could do it on her own and didn't need anyone. Now that Priest brought her back home, she thought she had live in baby sitters who could just watch and raise her kid while she chased after Reese's ass.

"I don't want to hear your mouth," Justice held her hand up before I could open my mouth.

"All I'm saying is that you need to stop allowing her to do this. It's not my home and I'm gonna mind my business. You'll get enough, and when you do, you'll put a stop to this."

"Yeah... Anyway, I haven't heard from her. I was on her Instagram the other day and she posted her job, so I assume she's working all the time."

"She promised that she wouldn't get into working those crazy hours again," I sighed.

"Yeah, well I don't want to pry into her business like she's a child. When she's ready to come around she'll come around."

"That's you, not me. We watch our sister damn near self-destruct and if that means I have to be in her business, then that's what I'm gonna do."

"I'll let the both of you handle that. I don't need Liberty barking on me and causing me stress. Besides her, what's going on with you?"

I put everything away, grabbed my sandwich, and sat down in the living room. Justice followed behind me and sat on the opposite couch. "I've been maintaining," my voice cracked.

"What is wrong?" Justice noticed the change in my demeanor and sat down beside me and started rubbing my back. "Tell me, Free," she pleaded.

"We went to the doctors and found out that the baby has a rare heart disease," I sobbed. "It's so rare that only one in ten thousand babies have it."

Justice's hand flew to her mouth. "Oh my. Why didn't you tell me?" she pulled me into her arms. I felt the tears from her eyes drop on the side of my face as she held onto me. "I'm so, so, so sorry, Free. You should have told me," she continued.

"I just wanted to process everything before telling everyone."

"Is it able to be fixed or cured?"

"No. He'll have to live with this disease for the rest of his life. Why is this happening to us? We thought everything was just settling down and now we're hit with this."

Justice continued to hug me as she sobbed. My sister could feel my pain and because we were so close, my pain was literally her pain. It was as if she was told that her baby had the same heart disease that my baby would have.

"God doesn't give you more than you can handle. I love you both so much and we're gonna be there for you and Samoor. We're a family and we'll be there for him no matter what."

"We have to head to Boston a little before I'm due so that the heart specialist can be there to perform surgery soon as he's born."

"Oh no, soon as he's born? Well, if you need me to come to Boston and help with the kids, I will."

"I know you will, and I love you for it. I have to speak to mommy so she can stay with the kids, so they don't miss school."

"You know mommy wouldn't mind stepping in so you could do what you need to when it comes to the kids."

"I know. Jus, I'm just so damn scared."

"I'm scared too, but we're used to fighting and this situation is no different. You fight hard, but when it comes to your chil-

dren you fight hard as fuck... Samoor is going to be good...
period."

"Period." I giggled as we hugged. This talk was something
that I needed in this moment. A quick trip to my sister's house
to feel her love and embrace. Justice may have been the
youngest, but she had this vibe about her that made you feel
like everything was going to be alright in life. I was glad that
she was my baby sister.

2

Staten

I don't hate any of y'all cause jealously ain't new to me – Nipsey Hussle

"Why you in here like this your home or something?" I asked Maliah, as she laid on the couch with a blanket wrapped around her, a bowl of soup in her hand and the remote in the other hand.

"It kind of is my second home. I'm barely home." She shrugged her shoulders. "It's something about being in the trap that makes me feel safe and at home." She laughed and continued to flip through the channels.

I finished running the last stack of money through the machine and checked my phone. Liberty still hadn't hit me back and I had called her two hours ago. Something was off with her and I wanted to know what was good with her. When she got out of rehab, you couldn't pay her to stay off me. Everything was going good and I thought we had finally stopped sinking in our relationship and shit would be cool for a minute. Besides Chanel, everything had been good between the both of us. Something changed with her and I tried hard to figure out what changed. She got distant again and wouldn't call unless I called her first. Then when I hit her to chill with me at the crib, she had all these excuses as to why she couldn't come through.

"Only you would feel like that," I laughed and went into the fridge to grab my leftover Chinese food. "You heard from Trac this week?"

"Nah, he's busy with Mariah. Mami wants to kill that man so damn bad," she snickered. "The only thing that stops her is that Mariah will hate her."

"I didn't think your mother would give a fuck about that." I pressed the heat button on the microwave and leaned against the counter.

"Believe it or not, she cares if we hate or love her. All mothers do. Even Messiah Garibaldi," she slurped up her ramen noodles. "Trac makes Mariah happy, so I don't see why she can't just leave them alone."

I grabbed my food and sat down on the couch beside her. This was the trap house where all the money was counted, so nobody was going to come through here. The only people that knew about it was Ghost, Messiah, and myself. The reason Maliah knew about it was because she had dropped some money off here a few times for Messiah. When she dropped by earlier, she told me she was here to pick up some money for her mother. That was three hours and two bowls of soup ago. Once she grabbed the blanket out the back room, I knew she wasn't about to leave no time soon. Being honest, I didn't mind her being here. While I counted up the money, she kicked it on the couch and kept me company. I plopped down beside her and propped my feet up on the coffee table as she continued to eat her soup. I looked over at her as she slurped her soup into her mouth without a care in the world.

"Your moms likes things her way or no way at all. You already know that," I smirked. Messiah was a woman that liked to have things her way or no way at all. Maliah knew that, so I didn't know why she was acting so shocked that her mother wanted Trac and Mariah broken up.

"Yeah, I know. Still, she can't control our lives forever. You can't help who you fall for," she sighed as she stared at me. I could feel the heat from her staring at me, but I ignored it.

"You sounding like you're in love or some shit," I laughed, and she placed her bowl down on the coffee table, then wrapped herself up in the blanket.

"I don't fall in love. I'm just saying... Mariah is in love with Trac, and my mother can't hold them back forever."

"And what about you? You still don't have no nigga you're entertaining?"

"I do, but he's taken at the moment." She cut her eyes at me.

"Since when that stopped you?"

She laughed. "I actually like his little girlfriend. They're cute for each other."

I shook my head and finished eating my food. "What else do you have planned for the day? You sitting up in here eating soup with this blanket like an old lady."

"Believe it or not, I was going to look up some properties."

"For what?"

"To live."

I mushed her leg. "Get the fuck outta here. I thought you said that you would never leave home?"

She shrugged. "Yeah, I did. I'm twenty-one and I don't need to be still living at home. Ain't no nigga gonna take me seriously still living with my parents."

"According to you, you wasn't chasing these niggas. I think you said the niggas you fuck with got their own place and shit," I joshed her memory.

"Like I said, what I look like living with my parents when

these niggas got their own cribs? With Munroe going away to college, I really don't want to be the only one left there."

"Understandable. Where you thinking about moving?"

"You got some for sale houses on your block," she joked.

"Yeah, get the fuck outta here. I don't need you as a neighbor." I waved her ass off. Maliah was wilding if she thought I wanted to live near her ass. "You need a condo anyway. It's your first time on your own... a house is too much responsibility for you."

She messed with her curls and stared at the TV. "Yeah, I'm weighing my options. How are you and Liberty?"

"Shit, you gotta ask her. I don't know what the fuck is going on with her. She been working a lot lately, so we haven't kicked it in a minute."

"And Chanel?"

"We got an appointment tomorrow. She's supposed to get her induction date tomorrow. I can't wait for my baby girl to be born."

"Everything with you and Chanel good?"

"Maliah, the fuck you being so damn nosey," I laughed. "Nah, we're good. She learned her place and we've been doing good. I'm just anxious as fuck for my daughter to be born. Chanel keeps texting me about feeling pressure, so I'm worried she's gonna deliver early."

"The baby should fall straight out with the way Chanel been fucking around Staten Island," she mumbled, and I tossed the pillow at her head. "What? Tell me that I'm lying?"

It was crazy how everyone knew how Chanel got down. The shit took me years to finally open my eyes and see how crazy my best friend was getting down. The thing about me and Chanel was that I was never in her business the way that she was always in mine. Chanel was always consumed with who I was fucking, and I could care less on who she was fucking with at the moment.

"That's my baby mama now. You got to chill." I nudged her.

"My bad. My bad. Liberty excited about the baby coming?"

"Nah. It doesn't excite her, and I get it. It's not her child."

I didn't force the baby on Liberty. Whenever me and Chanel had to handle something for the baby, we did it together without Liberty. The last thing I wanted was for her to feel like I was pushing the baby onto her. My daughter meant the world to me already and she hadn't even been born. I also knew that Liberty was still going through a lot, so I tried to keep from talking about the baby all the time. She never came out right and told me that she didn't want to hear about the baby, but I caught onto the eye rolls and mumbles whenever Chanel came around. A few times she complained about Chanel just popping over my house without calling to ask if it was cool to just come over. I was used to Chanel popping up whenever she wanted. Since we've been younger she's always done that, so it was the norm to me. Liberty acted like she couldn't live with Chanel coming around.

Even with all her complaining, she never started shit with Chanel and Chanel never started shit with her. I just needed the both of them to co-exist so that my daughter could come into this world healthy and not into a bunch of negative energy. Chanel didn't seemed bothered by anything that Liberty did, it was Liberty who was annoyed by her presence. Whenever I tried to talk to her about it, she brushed it off and tried to act like she was tired or didn't feel like discussing it.

"It doesn't matter that it's not her child. It's your child so she should be happy for you about it. I mean, this baby came into play before the both of you got together, right?" Maliah brought me back from my thoughts.

"Yeah, you right. She just been stressed lately and working and shit. I've been trying to give her space and shit."

"Well, you need to be her man and step up to the plate and

make sure she's good. Oh, and make sure she's not on that shit again," she made sure to add.

Liberty getting addicted to coke again was my worst fear. It was something that I thought about constantly. She didn't know that I would show up to her job and check her car while she was working to make sure she didn't have shit she wasn't supposed to her in her truck. If she knew she would be pissed, but it was better to know than not to know. Liberty had been a pro at hiding this from her family for years, so I knew she was good with hiding this shit. I didn't want to be the person she hid it from. If she found herself going back down that road, then we could make arrangements for her to get the help that she needed again. Putting the money up to check her back into rehab was nothing to me. Long as my baby was good, then I was good.

"I hear you." I stood up and stretched out. "Let me finish here so I could head home," I replied. Maliah's face frowned, but she recovered quickly by putting a smile on her face.

"You good?"

"Yeah, I'm fine. Why?"

"Nothing," I said and went back into the kitchen to finish handling business. It was something different about Maliah and I couldn't put my finger on it.

After I locked up the trap, I headed home so I could chill for a minute. Since Ghost stepped down, I had been running myself like a fucking slave trying to keep up with everything. I never realized just how much my brother did. I was trying to keep my street presence, but at the same time be the big man that met with the higher up niggas in the drug game. To me, I had been keeping up both, but I didn't know how much I was going to be able to play both roles. When Ghost decided to step back from the streets, he let it be known to me that he wouldn't be out there anymore. It was me who stepped up and was the face to the streets. I knew the time was coming to step away from the streets and have Trac handle that for me. Priest let me know that he was there for me and would continue to play his role, but he was also removing himself from the streets for the sake of his nieces, daughter, and Justice. Priest had never been the type to be out there on no wild shit.

He did what he had to do and was back in the crib with his nieces. It was Trac who was going to have to step up and make the noise that I had made for Ghost when I ran the streets. With me doing both, I barely had time for my own shit, and I wanted to make sure that I did. Liberty had her own shit going on, but I didn't have time to deal with her either, so it wasn't only her fault. Then with Chanel, I made the appointments that I could, but I knew it bothered her that I wasn't there as much as I should have been. At the end of the day, a nigga was only one person and I had to move smarter, not harder, and also make time for my family. My phone pulled me from my thoughts as I cruised and listened to Nipsey Hussle *Double Up*.

"What's good, Chanel?"

"Where are you? I'm at your house and you're not here."

"I had to handle some business... why you at my crib? Something wrong?"

"No... I just wanted to run the new names I picked out for the baby."

"New names? I thought you picked the names out weeks ago?" Chanel had changed our daughter's name about six times. At this point, I didn't even call her by a name until Chanel was a hundred percent sure. Hell, I probably wouldn't start calling her by her name until the birth certificate and social security was mailed to the house.

"I don't like those names anymore... oh, and my lease is up in the next three months. I'm going to re-new because I don't want to have to move with a new baby and she's due in a month."

"I hear all of that, but I don't want you living there. With me taking over shit for Ghost, niggas will try and come for the people I care about."

"If you think moving in with you is the best thing, then you're wrong. I'm not trying to hear Liberty's mouth about this."

"Nah, nah, nah... nothing like that. I'm gonna get up with my realtor and see if he can find you something that's near Mirror's townhouse. Ghost got that shit for a good price and it's nice as fuck."

"I don't want to live near Mirror." I could picture her turning her face up. It wasn't like Mirror wanted to live near her either.

"I don't care where you live, it's not gonna be in Port Richmond anymore. Like I said, I'll figure shit out and let you know what we came up with."

"And when are you coming home?"

"I'm pulling into the driveway now," I replied and ended the call.

Before I killed the engine and got out the car, I leaned my head back on the headrest and sighed. The plan was to move Chanel out of her apartment since I found out that she was pregnant. Too much shit happened, and I wasn't able to do that, but now that she was about to give birth, I had even more shit to do to make sure that she and my daughter was straight. I dialed Liberty's number and it went straight to voicemail. Tucking my phone into my pocket, I got out the car and hit the alarm before entering my crib. Chanel was sitting at the kitchen island flipping through a binder.

"The baby shower is next weekend and my dress still hasn't arrived," she complained.

I had no clue what was going on with the baby shower. All I knew was that I was paying out the ass like this shit was a fucking wedding or some shit. Anytime she needed the money for something, I would send it to her. Chanel and her mother both took the lead to plan this baby shower. My mother didn't want to be involved because she felt like Chanel should have come to her and asked her to be apart and she didn't. Chanel should have felt a way about my mother's feelings, but to her she didn't give a damn. All she cared about was the fact that it was about her and the baby. At this point, I didn't even know if my mother was going to come to the shower or not.

"You got a backup dress or something?"

"No. I was set on this dress and it hasn't even shipped yet." She continued to sit there and sulk.

"You better take your ass on Fashion Nova and grab something. If it's good enough for Cardi, it's good enough for your ass."

"This is my damn baby shower we're talking about, Shaliq. You think I'm supposed to just show up wearing some cheap Instagram outfit at my own baby shower?"

There wasn't going to be no reasoning with her, so I decided to switch the subject before I got pissed. "What's the new name?"

"I love this name and I'm not going to change it at all. It's Cherry."

"Hell nah. Chanel, I let you do any and everything with this pregnancy and never chimed in on anything. I draw the line at you trying to name my daughter after a stripper I fucked. Fuck outta here."

"A stripper you fucked. What are you talking about?"

"You don't even need to know all of that. Just know that my daughter's name isn't going to be no damn Cherry. Pick another name... case closed."

Chanel poked out that bottom lip thinking that I was going to change my stance on the name, and I wasn't. Out of all the names she could have picked, she picked a damn stripper name. Why the fuck did she think that I was going to be cool with that shit?

"Whatever. I was gonna name her Evie," she responded. "I like that name too."

"I'm cool with Evie. Long as her name isn't going to be fucking Cherry."

"I hear you, Shaliq. You don't have to keep bringing the shit up," she rolled her eyes. "Are you gonna ride with me to the shower in a limo?"

"A limo? Chanel, this shit ain't no damn prom. What the fuck is you thinking, man?"

"My daughter is hood royalty. You think I'm gonna throw some small shower? No, I'm throwing a shower fit for a Queen and Princess."

All I could do is shake my head because she was serious. While I was trying to keep a low profile, she was trying to let the entire hood know that she was carrying my baby. "You doing the most. How much have I spent on this baby shower?"

"Around fifty grand."

"Fifty grand?" I closed the fridge hard as shit.

"Stop being dramatic. That's not a lot and it would have been cheaper if your mother would have cooked."

"Your mama's hands broke?"

"My mama is gonna be by my side the whole event. You expect her to cook too?"

I leaned against the fridge and tried to get my thoughts together before I spoke. "My mom is good enough to cook for your event, but not to help you plan her future granddaughter's special day?"

"Why are you trying to make it seem like that? Grandparents cook for baby showers all the time."

"Nah, I'm not making it like anything. My mother tried to explain it to me, and I told her she was being dramatic. That's fucked up."

"Shaliq, I love your mother, so why do you think I would treat her like that? Come on, you're blowing this out of the water for no reason." She closed her binder and gathered her purse. "Whenever you stop trying to take things personal, then we'll finish discussing this." She turned and headed to the door. "Oh, you scared me. Hey," I heard Chanel say.

"Hey."

"Oh, and before I forget...." her voice trailed off as she dug into her binder and pulled out an envelope. "Here's your invitation to the baby shower."

"I didn't think I needed one," Liberty replied.

"Oh, everyone needs one. The only people that don't need one is my baby daddy, my parents and Shaliq's mother."

Liberty looked at me and then looked back at Chanel. "Cool."

"Oh, and don't bring a guest. That invitation is only for you. I know you have sisters and stuff," she made sure to add.

"Hell, I might not even be there," she replied and walked by her and into the kitchen.

"Let me know please. There's a bunch of people that want an invitation." Chanel continued to the door and left.

Soon as the door closed, I knew I was about to hear Liberty's mouth. "Why every time I come over she's always here? Damn. Can I not see her for once?" she barked. "I'm tired of always having to hear this bitch whenever I come to see you."

"You acting like I called her over here or something. When I came home she was here already," I replied and attempted to grab a water for the second time.

"Why does she even have a key? I don't even have a key, but this bitch can come and go whenever she pleases without any issues. I'm tired of always seeing her when I come over. Chanel acts like she doesn't have any boundaries and you allow her to move like that."

After everything I handled today, this wasn't what I wanted to come home to hear. "You want me to take the key from her? Ight, I'll get it from her tomorrow."

"No, I want you to take the key because you want to take it. I shouldn't have to tell you what to do, Staten. She shouldn't have a key to your place when you have a girlfriend."

"What happened today? You real aggravated and just walked through the door five minutes ago."

"No, I walked in the door thinking I can spend some time with my man, maybe even get some dick and I'm met with the constant reminder that you got Chanel pregnant and she's always going to be a part of my life," she spat and leaned against the counter.

"You were cool with it."

"Because it's for you. Am I excited? Not really. It has nothing to do with the baby either. I know that Chanel is dramatic and will use that baby to insert herself into our relationship."

"I would never let that happen. My daughter is my daughter and me and Chanel's relationship is separate from that. What we have is important to me, you hear me?"

"I'm just so confused and annoyed about everything."

"The fuck you so confused about?"

"You claim you let her know what it is when it comes to the both of us, yet she still running around with the key to your place and she just lets herself in this house without even knocking. The last time we were about to fuck, she walked right into the damn house. Why should I, as your girlfriend, have to live like that?"

"You shouldn't," I agreed.

"Then why does she still have a key and still is able to say whatever she wants? Sometimes I just don't know..." she allowed her voice to trail off.

"Don't know what?"

"About us. Chanel is always going to be around because she's your child's mother, but I don't know if this is something I want to deal with."

"That's not fair, Liberty. I told you from jump what it was, and you decided to stick around. My feelings are invested in this shit too."

"The baby shower she is throwing is a fucking whole big thing. Everyone is talking about Chanel and Staten. What about me? Where do I fit into your life with her? Is this how it's going to be whenever she throws something for your daughter? Am I supposed to be the one waiting on an invitation or I can't attend? I'm just sick of this shit, man." She walked over to the window with her arms over her head.

"You know I'm not gonna make you come with no fucking invitation so why do you even pay Chanel any mind? You know she does shit just to get under your skin."

"That's the thing. Do I want to share my life with a bitch that does stuff just to get under my skin? I'm a grown ass woman and feel like I have to stoop down to high school level whenever she's around. I just don't have the energy for the shit."

Liberty had never spoke about how she felt before. I always saw the eye rolls and sucking her teeth, but she never came out right and spoke about how she felt. I walked over to her and wrapped my arms around her waist, then placed a kiss on her lips.

"You know I love the shit out of you, right?"

"Uh huh," she replied.

"I'll talk to Chanel and fix this, ight?"

"Yeah, and nothing will happen like the last few times you've spoken to her. I'm on my period and tired," she yawned. Liberty wiggled out of my arms and then went back into the kitchen.

"You worked today? I called you and got the voicemail."

"My phone has been off all morning. Yeah, and I had to hear about how many people got invitations to Chanel's baby shower at work. It's like high school working there," she sulked.

"Go shower and lay in the bed. I'm gonna order us something and we can chill and watch some movies until we fall asleep."

Liberty sighed. "Okay." She finally agreed and stalked off toward the bedroom. I watched as she closed the bedroom door behind her and grabbed my phone and went onto the patio to smoke a blunt. Having two women at each other's neck all the time was something that would cause a nigga to drink. This blunt was going to have to do, because at this moment I felt like everything was going wrong for me.

Maliah

"MALIAH, why you always showing up when I'm trying to get some dick? It's like you have some kind of weird ass sensor or something," Mariah complained as I pushed my way into her condo.

I hadn't been to sleep in two days and all I wanted was to spend some time with my twin sister. "Nice to see you too, Mariah. I mean, damn. I ain't seen you in over two weeks," I barked and took a seat in her living room.

Mariah's condo overlooked the New York harbor. You could see the Staten Island ferry making its usual commute between Manhattan and Staten Island. Off in the distance, you could see Hoboken, New Jersey as well. My parents paid out the ass for her to have this condo directly on the water front. Her unit was the only one with a balcony and on the top floor. My father was the one who pushed and actually went through with purchasing this place. My mother refused because she didn't want Mariah to leave home. It was my father who put his foot down and made sure that Mariah got a nice condo that she actually wanted.

"I'm sorry, but you're always popping over at the wrong time. What's up?" she pulled her silk robe closed and stared at me.

"You can go and finish up. I'll be right here."

I heard laughing and turned to see Trac buckling his jeans. "You wild. I'm not about to smash while you out here. I keep telling you that I can hook you up with my cousin, Maliah," Trac offered like he always did.

"And, I'm gonna tell you that I don't need you to hook me up with no nigga," I spat and kicked my sneakers off and got comfortable on the blush colored couch.

"Ma, I'm gonna see you tonight. I love you, ight?" Trac pulled her to him by the waist and she stood on her toes to kiss him on the lips.

"See you later, baby," she said in this baby ass voice as she walked him to the door. I rolled my eyes as I watched him kiss her lips a few times.

"Closed the damn door, Mariah. Damn!" I hollered.

"You rude as hell," she snapped and finally closed the damn door and came and sat on the couch opposite from the one I was occupying. "What the hell do you want?" she crossed her legs and leaned back on the couch.

"If you're gonna be mean, you can go in there and finish whatever the both of you started, then come out here and talk to me."

"Maliah, you're always cock blocking," she whined and put her hands over her face. "What do you need, Twin? What is so important that you needed to come banging on my door?"

"Mami wouldn't want him here. How you know I didn't come save you?"

"Mami doesn't come to my house. When she does, she calls and lets me know to leave the door unlocked."

"Maybe I need to start moving like her... cause you left me in that damn hall for over six minutes," I looked at my Rolex.

"Maliah! What the hell do you want?" she raised her voice and stared at me. "You're beating around the bush, just go on and tell me."

"I think I'm falling for Staten," I admitted.

Mariah's mouth opened wide as she stared at me. "Staten Davis? Uncle's little brother? Are you fucking kidding me?"

I covered my face with the throw pillow and tried to avoid eye contact with my sister. She was squealing and tossing stuff for me to look her in the eyes. "Why you being so extra? Did I do all of this when you told me about Trac?"

"Trac is different, Maliah. We didn't grow up around him... Mami would surely kill the both of you if she ever found out."

I removed my curly tresses out of my face and looked at my twin. "She's not going to find out."

Mariah made the zipping motion across her lips as she stared at me. "So, how did you both start messing around?"

"Huh?"

"Messing around? How did it start?"

"We're not. He doesn't even know how I feel about him," I admitted.

Mariah waved me off. "You basically have a crush on him. It'll fade away." She went into the fridge and grabbed some freshly squeezed peach juice. "What else is going on?"

I sat up and put my feet onto the floor. "I'm being serious, Riah. I feel something for this man and it's not a joke."

She turned around with her glass of juice. "And what do you want me to tell you? Staten is like family and you're telling me that you're falling for him. Mami damn sure hasn't approved of Trac, do you think she will for Staten?"

"I'm not worried about Mami right now. As your sister, all I'm asking for is for you to be there and talk to me. I don't want logical, I just want my sister," I admitted.

My feelings for Staten had always been there. Yeah, he was like family, but I never looked at him like that. Once I grew older, we did a lot of business together and were always together. I couldn't help but feel like I was the woman that he was supposed to be with. At twenty-one, I knew he wasn't looking for a young dumb chick, and that wasn't the vibe I was coming to him with either. A lot of chicks my age played games and liked to play that teasing game with men, but I knew what I wanted and had no problem going for it. Staten was what I wanted, but I didn't know how to confront him. He was with Liberty and I didn't want to step on another woman's toes.

Mariah sighed. "Fine. When did you start feeling like this?"

"Last year."

"A whole year you've been feeling this man and haven't said anything? Is this why you refuse to date anyone?"

"First of all, all these niggas are fucking scum. They keep forgetting that I'm a Queen and haven't come correct. Fuck I look like fucking a nigga that live at home with his mama?" I spat with disgust.

The problem with the men my age was that they were too immature. They were so busy hanging out, bragging, and not worried about getting money. I wanted a nigga that was out in the street as much as I was. Fuck I looked like grinding harder than my man? It wouldn't work because I would always feel like I was bringing more to the table than he was. I tried talking to guys my age and we never connected. Their conversation wasn't worth sitting over dinner and pretending to be interested in. Mariah lucked up with Trac because he was a rare breed. You could tell that he wasn't with the shit and wanted to come up in the game. The niggas he hung with were all clowns, which is why he was barely with them. Now that he was one of Staten's second hands, you could tell that he took the role serious. I wanted a nigga to run the streets and then come home to me. Shit, we can meet each other at the door on our way into the crib. Was that too much to ask for?

Staten was all of that and then some more. He stepped into

his brother's position and ran it with an iron fist. He didn't give a damn about putting on for these lames out here in Staten Island. Even though he took over Ghost's position, he was still in the trap counting money and bagging up work, even though he didn't have to. When I didn't have things to do, I would go and sit in the trap with him for hours just soaking up the knowledge that he had. A man that could teach me something was a man that I wanted. It was just something about Staten Davis that made me want to toss my panties to the floor and jump right on him.

"Staten is in love with Liberty, so how do you think you and him are going to work out? You gonna take that girl's man?"

"I'm not going to break them up. It's not my place and I'm definitely not breaking up a happy home."

"Good. Now, you need to tell Mami to have someone else work around him."

"You ready to come out of retirement and do my job? You're the only other person besides Munroe. Since Munroe is going to college, you're going to have to take over my spot."

"Why did she have to go and want to be smart?"

"Daddy actually made her go to college."

"For what?"

"He doesn't want that life for her. Munroe is too smart to be in the streets anyway... she needs to go and get that degree and be something."

"I'm smart. Why does she get that option, but my only option was to run the streets? I'm tired of killing and dealing with drugs, Liah. I want to live a normal life, start a business and be rid of this game... Mami chose this life, not us," she vented. "Don't you ever wonder what it's like to sleep without having flashbacks?"

I shrugged. "I haven't had a full night's sleep in years, it's normal to me. I like this street shit, Mariah. We were born for this."

"*You* were born for this shit. I didn't ask for this life." She stood up and paced the living room. "I wake up in cold sweats and screaming because of some of the shit we've done or witnessed. Thankfully Trac is there to hold me through the night. Everyone talks about the glory of being feared, respected, the money and having the hood royalty, but no one ever talks about the night terrors, looking over your back or not being able to go to a simple house party because of who your parents are. I'm so sick of living like this, Mariah."

Everything that my twin said was the truth. The streets didn't have any loyalty, yet we all were very loyal to the streets. I saw the streets take my god sister away without a blink of an eye. I struggled with paranoia because of the streets and night terrors were just the cherry on top. I understood why Mariah didn't want to be in the streets anymore and I had no other option other than to support her. She had been vocal about stepping back and my mother always thought it was a phase she was going through. Now, she saw how Mariah fell back and didn't deal with anything that had to do with the family's business. Our father supported us in any and everything that we wanted to do. Mariah not handling business didn't bother him at all, but it bothered my mother to the core. It was the reason she had this hate built up in her heart for Trac. While she was so busy thinking that Trac was the reason for Mariah's sudden departure from the streets, she didn't realize, or maybe even didn't care to learn that this was Mariah's decision. Trac loved Mariah whether she was in the streets or holding it down at home.

"You're getting upset. We don't need to talk about this right now," I told her. From the way she was pacing, and her breathing was getting heavier, I knew this wasn't what she wanted to discuss, and we didn't have to.

"I'm going to therapy," she announced. "I've been going for the past month and it really does help me... you should go."

"Mariah, what are you telling this lady?"

"Nothing. I just tell her things that I struggle with. I'm not stupid, Maliah." She got upset and plopped back down on the couch. "All I want to be is Trac's wife."

"It's cool to be his wife, but that's all you want to be? Mami has the best of both worlds." My mother had always been my role model. She had her flaws, but I always admired how she was able to have both her family and the streets. That was what I wanted. I never wanted to sit back and be someone's wife. I wanted to stand beside my man and run our empire together.

"Daddy wanted more children... you know that? Mami went and had her tubes tied and burned because she refused to take more time away from running our empire," she told me. "You know they were separated for a bit when we were younger? Daddy is always gone because he can't stand to be home with Mami. Do you want to live a life like that?"

"Stop lying," I told her and put my sneakers back on. "Mami and Daddy are happy together. They're goals to these couples in the streets."

"Yeah, until you're living on the inside and see everything unscrambling. I don't doubt that Daddy loves Mami, but I do know that he wanted more kids and Mami took that from him. There's so much that we don't know that they battle in their marriage behind closed doors, Mariah. All I'm saying is that my future husband can have this street shit. I just want to be his peace when he comes through our door."

"Yeah, all of that sounds good for you. I want to be out there handling business just like my man."

"Just because we look alike doesn't mean that we have to think alike. As far as you and Staten, just be careful with that situation. You put on this hard exterior, but you're sensitive and I don't ever want you to get hurt."

I walked over to her and hugged her tightly. "I love you, Mariah."

"Love you too. Be safe out there, Liah," she told me as I grabbed an apple out the fruit bowl and headed out of the front door.

Our conversation had gotten way too deep and I needed to take a drive and think of everything she had laid out on the table. I knew the game had its flaws, but it was all I had known. My mother started teaching us the game when we were young. It was all we had heard and learned about. I couldn't wait until I was older to run with everything my mother had taught us. Mariah had always been into stuff other than what Mami was teaching. She excelled in every test our mother presented us with, but I always knew her heart wasn't in this like it was for me. I loved making my mother proud. To me, my parents had the perfect marriage and they were what I aspired to be when I found the right man.

I knew Mariah didn't believe that what I felt for Staten was real, but it was real. Staten needed a woman to stand by his side and that was going to ride for him. I couldn't continue to live at home while trying to be the woman that he needed me to be. Having my own place was an important part of the process and it was something I needed to get in order as soon as possible. I sat in my car and leaned my head back to process everything me and Mariah had just spoke about. I loved how we were able to have deep conversations without getting into an argument. We would yell, disagree, but at the end of our conversation we would still come together and still have love for one another. I didn't agree with how my sister chose to live her life, but I respected it. Like she said, just because we looked alike didn't mean we had to share the same views on life. I put the car and drive and headed home so I could shower and take a quick nap.

"MALIAH, you've been asleep since yesterday afternoon... is there something you're not telling me?" I heard my mother's voice as I opened one eye and stared outside. The sun was shining right inside the room. I could see the pool's reflection on my ceiling.

I sat up, yawned, and stretched before I responded. This was another reason that I needed to move out. My mother didn't believe in privacy. She would waltz into any room without a knock and didn't find a problem with it.

"I was tired and haven't slept in a while." I continued to yawn and climb out of my California king bed. This bed was far too big for me, still I slept on every inch of this enormous bed.

"Well, you need to get with Staten. He has to take a trip soon and I think he wants to go over the details with you. How's the trap in West Brighton?"

"Running. Good. I was over there the other day," I confirmed.

"The other day isn't good enough, Maliah. You should be riding by and keeping them niggas on their toes. Instead, you're in here sleeping the day away. Get up and get to business," she raised her voice slightly.

"I'm gonna go after I finish eating," I told her and went into my bathroom. As I expected, she was right on my heels with her signature face. It wasn't mad, sad or anything. My mother was stoic.

"Your sister doesn't want to run the game and now you want to stuff your face before heading out and Munroe wants to go to college. Where did I go wrong? Do you know me and Jayla were running the game at your age?"

"Yeah, and I also know you slipped and fell in love, then got pregnant with us. Ma, nobody is perfect, and the game will be there whether I stop to feed myself or not."

"Hurry it up, Maliah," she advised and left the bathroom. I heard my bedroom door close soon after and had a sigh of relief.

I showered, dressed, and was on my way out the door with a

breakfast sandwich from the chef. I pressed the start button in my car and pulled out of our gates quickly. While eating my sandwich and steering with my thighs, I put in the address to Staten's trap house in Tottenville. My mother told me where he was expecting me on my way out. While she told our pilot to fuel up the jet, I was trying to load up on any and everything the chef was trying to feed me. It was then when she stopped focusing on her call and made me leave to meet Staten. The chef handed me a breakfast sandwich on my way out. I didn't know what meeting Staten wanted to hold and what I had to do with it. With how many things I had to oversee a day, I didn't need to take on anything else.

I pulled up to the curb of the white single story stucco house. Killing the engine, I hopped out and made my way to the front door. With the amount of cameras he had around, I knew he saw me pull up. The front door opened, and he stood there without his shirt on. I licked my lips and then pulled myself together before he noticed. I'm thankful he didn't notice because he was too busy on the phone.

"Nah, she not coming with no damn invitation. I paid for the damn shower, Chanel," he barked and closed the door behind me. He pulled me into a one arm hug and then walked further into the house. "Fuck all that shit. I don't want to hear shit about what needs to be done or how you're doing things. Fix this shit, Chanel. I swear!" he barked once more before he ended the call.

I stood by the counter looking through the dozen of unopened text messages from niggas I had no interest in dating. "I don't want to talk about it."

"Wasn't going to ask."

"Word? It's like that?"

"I mean.... People like their space and I don't want to pry, especially if you don't want to talk about it. I'm not in the business of getting into people's shit."

"Oh word? Yet, you always in my shit." He smirked. It was that smirk that I loved so damn much. He could charm a damn gold fish with that smile.

"Yeah, when I want to be. Right now I don't care what selfish shit Chanel is up to," I quickly replied.

Chanel was selfish, spoiled, and annoying. Everyone knew it and nobody said anything because they knew that she was Staten's best friend. She used his name to get away with a lot of shit. With her being older than me, I couldn't stand how immature she acted. She was a whole ass grown woman with a baby in her stomach, yet she was acting like a damn child.

"Liberty pissed with me."

"What you do?"

"Why I gotta do something?"

"Cause you're Staten." I laughed and jumped up on the kitchen island. "What happened?" I added.

"I don't know she been real different lately. All she do is work, and when she's off, she goes and visits with her son."

"Okay..."

"When she's not working or with her son, she never wants to chill. She be talking about she at the gym or gotta run errands or some shit."

"Maybe she just needs her space."

"Space? For what? It's not like I be all in her space and shit. I barely got time to wipe my own ass and shit. All I want to do is spend time with my shorty."

"I hear you. Maybe you should go by her apartment and surprise her or something... do something to spice y'all shit up."

As much as I wanted Staten, I didn't want him while he was with Liberty. His feelings for Liberty was real and true. I wanted him to fix it with her because if he didn't, I knew that it would hurt him. The last thing I wanted was for him to be hurt – again. When

Liberty went into rehab, he was going down a spiral. The man that I thought had so much strength, broke down. He broke and I never wanted him to feel like that again. So, if I had to put my feelings aside to make sure that he never hurt like that again, I would.

"Lib ain't never fucking home. I don't be having time to sit around and wait for her to come home. I know I be working mad hard and shit, but I'm doing this to secure our future."

"Our?"

"Yeah, me and Lib. I want to make that woman my wife. She works all these hours and I want her to quit and be my wife. She should be able to visit her son all the time, not when she's off from work. I want her to shop in the mall in the middle of the day with no limit. Her last name should be Davis," he explained. As I stared into his eyes, I could see the love he held for her. When he spoke her name, it was almost like he was saying it delicately.

"I see. Then make the time, Staten. You want y'all to work, then make the shit work. You need to be there and step up. I know there's shit Liberty needs to do on her end, but I'm not talking to her right now, I'm talking to you."

"I hear you. Give me a hug, you always coming with the real. Remind me of your damn mother." He chuckled as we shared a hug.

"You're the homie... I'm always gonna be here."

"And I appreciate you for it." He kissed me on the cheek and then took a step back. "Now dealing with business. I need to head back to Belize and check shit out."

"And?"

"I need you to ride out with me. Your mother thinks it's time for you to learn about what we do over there."

"She told me that you needed me. Not once did she mention that this was going to be some damn lesson or something."

"All lessons are needed. Your sister stepped back, so it's up to you to learn everything and what we do out in Belize."

"Whatever. When do we leave?"

"In a few weeks. I need to make sure everything will be good when I leave. We're gonna be out there for two weeks."

"Two weeks?"

"You think you gonna learn everything in five minutes? Nah, you need two weeks and then some, but we'll start with two weeks."

I sulked because the two weeks I would be gone would equal to that much work that needed to be done. There was only one person I could trust to take over while I was gone and that was Mariah. The thing is, would she step in for me?

3

Justice
Your friends proud when they see you fucking with me – Nipsey Hussle

"Baby girl is in there doing amazing!" My doctor beamed as she helped me sit up on the table. Priest was smiling so wide I'm sure his damn teeth would drop onto the floor next.

"That's wonderful. I've been so nervous about her lately. She doesn't move as much as she used to."

"Well, there's not much room in there anymore. She probably moves, but while you're asleep or not paying too much attention. She's fine... don't worry too much."

"Thank you. I've just been worried since finding out about my nephew's heart condition. I just pray to have a healthy baby."

"No more worries, Justice. I've been your OB/GYN since the beginning of your pregnancy. You've come this far. Keep the positive energy, okay?"

"I keep telling her this," Priest stood up and rubbed my stomach.

I sighed because I was a big ball of worry. All I did was worry about Yasmine and if everything would be alright with her delivery. Free didn't think her baby would have a heart condition and then look what happened. As much as everyone told me to calm down, I couldn't. It was my last thought before I closed my eyes and the first thought when I woke up. How could I stop worrying about something that meant the world to me? Yasmine meant so much to me and she didn't know how much I needed her. She came at a time where I was so confused about life. I knew I loved Priest and wanted to be with him, yet I was so confused with where my next step in life would be. Then, I got pregnant with her and I knew everything was going to be alright. All of a sudden, my next move wasn't as important as her and Priest. This family is something I wanted and losing another baby wasn't an option. I truly don't think I would be able to get through that if it happened to me this far along in my pregnancy.

"I'm sorry for making an appointment. I just needed to know."

"You're fine, Justice. I understand your concerns. Let's try and keep our visits down some, okay?" she smiled as she handed me a warm wash cloth to wipe the jelly off my stomach.

"Okay," I agreed.

"Thanks again, Doctor." Priest shook her hand and she exited out of our exam room. I wiped the jelly off my stomach and then got down from the table with his help to pull my dress down. "You gotta stop this worrying, Justice. I drove all the way over here from Stapleton because you had me scared as fuck."

"I didn't mean to scare you. I'm sorry," I apologized. "I was at the center trying to pick the final colors for the painters and I jiggled my stomach and she didn't kick back. Ro, she always kicks back when I do that."

He pulled me into a hug. "I know you're scared. I'm scared too and pray every day over you and my baby. You have to stop getting yourself so worked up. That shit ain't good for you or Yasmine. Plus, she keeps you up all night anyway, so she's just sleeping."

"Use to."

"Huh?"

"She used to keep me up. Now I don't feel her."

"Babe, do you realize how knocked out you be? I be trying to get you to the other side, and you be knocked the fuck out. You probably so deep in your sleep that you don't feel her moving inside of you."

He had a point. Still, I wasn't convinced. "Well, your daughter is hungry so what are we getting to eat?"

"Meet at our favorite restaurant by the beach."

"What's the occasion? We always go there during occasions."

"A healthy and happy baby," he kissed me on the lips and held my hand as we exited out of the office.

I didn't plan to end up at the doctor's office today when I woke up, I had plans to go on about my day and have a good day. I knew Priest was probably getting tired of me worrying, making unnecessary doctor visits, and keeping him up late because of a bad dream I had. I wish I wasn't this way and I could have a carefree pregnancy, but I couldn't. I had lost too much for me to sit back and not worry about any and everything that happened when it came to my daughter.

"Drive safe, I'm right behind you," he told me as he closed the door behind me. I pulled out of the parking lot and he followed behind me. I pressed Liberty's name as I drove to the restaurant.

"Hey," she answered. Liberty always sounded dry when I spoke to her on the phone. I never got an overly hyped greeting when I called her.

"What's up with you? I haven't spoken to you since you were at my house."

"Is there a rule that says that I have to call and check up on you and Freedom?" she snapped, and I looked at myself in my rearview.

"Ouch, who pissed you off?"

"Nobody. I'm just tired of everyone expecting me to check up on them. I have my own shit going on too," she vented.

"Lib, I don't expect you to check up on me. Believe it or not, I want to hear from my big sister from time to time."

I heard her stifle a laugh. "Sorry. I just had a long day today and just got a minute to myself," she explained.

"You're fine. I just wanted to pop in and see how you're doing."

"Working and trying to be there for Chance whenever I can."

"How's Chance doing? I called last week and got the machine, so I left a message for him and auntie."

"He's good. It's baseball season so he's doing that half the time."

"Okay, cool. How are you and Staten?"

"I don't know. I barely see him and when I do Chanel is always tagging behind him."

I had heard that Chanel's baby shower was going to be a huge event. Anyone who was anyone was invited. "I heard about her shower."

"Can you believe that bitch told me that I can only come with an invitation and I couldn't bring anyone?"

"Are you serious?"

"Yep. I'm tired of her and Staten allows the shit too. He does nothing to stop the shit she does. Honestly, I'm sick of the both of them," she sucked her teeth.

"Wait, so he doesn't stop her and he's making you go to the baby shower with the invitation?"

"Girl no. He told me he was going to handle it. Still, I don't think I'm going to go."

"You think he'll be pissed?" I asked as I turned into the parking lot of the restaurant. I found a parking spot and watched Priest pull in right next to me.

"I don't care if he'll be pissed. His baby mama is fucking annoying and wants to fuck him. I'm sick of being the third damn wheel when it comes to their situation," she sighed. "Anyway, what are you doing?"

"Me and Priest are grabbing some food," I replied.

"Well, you go and grab some food and feed my niece and I'll talk to you soon," she tried to rush me off the phone. "Why did you get quiet?"

"Because I worry about you," I admitted.

"There is no need to worry about me, I'm fine. I'm going to soak in the tub and get ready for work tomorrow," she tried to add some cheer in her voice.

"Alright. Talk to you soon," I told her and ended the call.

Priest tapped on my window and I unlocked my doors. I watched as he held my door open and reached his hand out to help me out the car. "I'm dying for some grilled salmon," he licked his lips as he closed my door behind him.

"I just want some food. We're hungry," I laughed.

South Fin Grill was one of my favorite restaurants in Staten Island. Priest took me here at least three times a month, and since I've been pregnant we've been here even more. It was right on the beach. We were seated at a table that gave us a beautiful view of the beach and the Verrazano bridge. Priest held the chair out for me, and I slid inside the seat and smiled as he sat down across from me.

The hostess handed us the menus. "Your waitress will be with you shortly," he said and pranced off toward the front of the restaurant.

"You look beautiful today, baby," Priest complimented, like

he always did. Priest always made me feel like the most beautiful woman in the world. My confidence was always on a high because this man built me up like a construction worker.

"Thank you, boo. Besides this little doctor visit, how was your day today?" I decided to switch any conversation about the baby. We often got so wrapped up into the baby that we forgot to talk about *us* from time to time.

"It was good. I had to handle a few things, but other than that everything was good... Do you have a date you want to open the center? I know you're still picking the colors, but have you thought about a grand opening date?"

The center was something that I took pride in. I was excited that my dream was finally going to happen. This was something that I had wanted for a while and now I was this close to making everything happen. Everyone was hired and I handpicked everyone to work in my center. I also had a few schools in the area interested in partnering for an afterschool program. All in all, I was so excited about everything that was happening. Children needed a safe place where they could come to after school where they could do their homework and enjoy a snack before heading home for the day. I wanted to make this a place where all children felt safe to come to. It was needed here on Staten Island and I was glad that I was going to be able to provide something back to my community.

"I'm thinking sometime after the baby is born. I don't want to open it while I'm pregnant. My mind is always on Yasmine and the center. I want to be fully focused on the center."

"There's no rush, baby. I'm just asking because I know you're excited to get it opened."

"I am. I just want to make sure that everything is handled home before opening. I know wants it gets opened that I'll be pretty busy."

"I bet you will." He winked at me. "You heard from Kiss today?" he questioned.

Kiss had called me earlier, but she had called me to tell me that her friend was going to watch Zamari," I informed him.

Kiss was all over the place these days and I never knew what was going on with her and Zamari. All I knew is that she asked me to watch him when she didn't want to be bothered or wanted to chase after her friends, then got him from me when she wanted to be a mother again. I didn't judge Kiss, well I tried hard not to judge her. She was a young mother trying to do her best. Yet, I was tired of her always thinking that me and her uncle were live in sitters so she could rip and run the streets and be young again.

"She always dropping him off with some fucking body," he slightly raised his voice. "Why the fuck does she never have her child?"

I shrugged my shoulders. "She's young, Ro. You know what you were doing around her age," I sighed.

"Yeah, doing what needed to be fucking done. I was fucking raising her ass. Even before my sister's sickness was worse, I was still holding it down and raising the girls. Kiss wanted to hide and have this baby, so she needs to raise her child." He gulped down the glass of water in front of him.

"Welcome to *South Fin Grill*, my name is Lavern, can I start you both off with something to drink?"

Priest choked on his water and then slowly looked up at the waitress. She was a brown skin woman with long brown hair that touched her shoulders. She had a mole on the corner of her lip. The woman was beautiful, there was no denying that. Seeing how Priest was staring at this woman like he had seen a ghost let me know that he knew her from somewhere.

"Roshon? Oh my god!" The woman gasped as she put her small notepad up to her mouth in shock.

The shocked expression still hadn't wiped away from Priest's face. "Baby, you alright?" I cleared my throat.

He put the glass down and grabbed my hand from across

the table. "Yeah, I'm good." He turned his attention to the wait-ress. "Lavern, damn when did you move back?"

"I've been back for a few months now. How have you been?"

"Word. I've been good. So you working here?"

She looked down at her uniform and giggled. "Yeah, and I work at a bar in Port Richmond at night.... You know to pay the bills."

I coughed and both of them looked my way. While they were looking I made sure to put my hand over the top of my stomach so she could see that I was pregnant and hungry as hell. "This is my girlfriend, Justice," Priest introduced me to her. "Baby, this is my *friend*, Lavern."

I didn't like how he said the word friend. It was like he choked it out or something. Even when he mentioned friend, the woman's face told me otherwise. "Hi, how are you? I would like to order." I was tired of this awkward stare down between the both of them.

She flipped out her notepad. "Of course. I'm so sorry. What can I get for you both?" she looked at Priest first, then her eyes found their way over to me.

"I'll do the brine roasted chicken breast. I'll also take some lemonade as well as my drink," I replied.

"The pan roasted salmon and some bourbon," Priest ordered.

"I'm so happy that I ran into you," she put her hand on his shoulder and smiled down at him. What bugged me out was that Priest was showing all his damn teeth in his mouth with that smile he was showcasing. "I'll put your orders in and grab your drinks," she lightly tapped her notepad on the table before she walked away.

"What the hell and who was that?" I leaned across the table and harshly whispered. He was still looking her way when she left the table. When he turned my way, he jumped back once he noticed my face.

"Ma, why you looking like that?"

"Because you haven't told me who that woman was and why you're so smitten and smiling at her?"

"You bugging. I'm not smitten. That's my home girl, Lavern." He tried to wave it off like it wasn't anything. His whole expression changed when he heard the woman introduce herself, then he looked up at her and his voice was stuck in his throat. This was more than a homegirl.

"Home girl, huh? Why haven't I heard about this home girl then?"

"Do you need to know about every home girl that I know? I know you haven't told me about every nigga or friend you got or had," he snapped.

"Okay."

"Don't shut down on me because I snapped on you," he demanded, and I nodded my head. There was nothing left for us to talk about. If he said that this was his home girl, then I had no other choice but to believe that... Well, until he proved otherwise.

"Whew, if he didn't take his nap I was going to rip my damn hair out," Kiss sighed as she plopped down on the stool in the kitchen.

I took the banana bread I had baked out of the oven and shook my head. Zamari was cutting teeth and his mother didn't know how to handle him. Instead of finding him relief for his teeth coming in, she would rather stick him inside his bedroom to take a nap. It was Kiss's child, so I learned to keep my mouth shut and let her do what works for her as a parent. Kiss's problem was that she thought she knew everything and never wanted to listen. It was like soon as she hit eighteen, had her baby, and had moved out she thought she knew everything about life. There were times when I decided to ignore her and let her think she knew everything about life.

"You need to get him those teething toys," I replied as I started to fill the dish washer with the dishes I had used when making my bread.

"Yeah, I need to go and get me some... you okay?" she asked.

Usually, I would tell her that I was fine and just keep my issues to myself, but right now I needed someone to talk to. Since Freedom was dealing with her own life issues and Liberty was too busy with hers, Kiss was the only person I had that could lend me a listening ear.

"I'm not." I leaned on the counter. "Ro ran into his home girl, Lavern. I don't know... I just keep thinking about it," I sighed.

"Lavern?" Kiss damn near screamed out. "His home girl?"

It was clear that Kiss knew something from the way she damn near hollered this woman's name and then said home girl like it was a question. "What do you know, Kiss?"

She sighed and then turned to look at me. "Lavern and Ro were close. Like, I mean she was the love of this man's life. He never speaks about her because I think it hurt when she moved away."

"Since he doesn't speak about her, you need to speak about her and let me know what is the deal between them."

We moved into the living room where Kiss laid across the couch and I sat in the opposite couch. "Lavern was Ro's first love. They were dating when my mother was still alive. She has been there through everything, but they grew apart after he had to drop out of college. Then you know... he got involved in the streets. She went to live abroad in London and then their relationship kind of faded. He never talks about her, but she was a big part of his life," she explained.

I knew something else was up with this woman and Priest had been acting funny ever since we had dinner there a few nights ago. Things weren't bad, but I could feel the disconnect since he ran into that woman. From what Kiss said, she was the love of his life. You never got over the love of your life, especially the way they seemed to have ended. Priest had to grow up overnight and become a man for his nieces, so I could see where his focus shifted from school to bringing money in. I also could see why his relationship would have never worked because of the sudden shift in his responsibilities. My question was why he would lie or downplay who this woman was to me? It wasn't like I wasn't understanding and couldn't understand that she was a past lover. If I could be understanding with his situation he once had with Marisol, then I could be understanding about a woman that was in his life way before me and him got together.

"I knew it was something about that woman."

"Ro is such a square so I'm sure he won't cheat on you or nothing like that," she added, which didn't make me feel better.

"I wasn't thinking that he would cheat on me. I'm just worried that he didn't tell me about her when we saw her in the restaurant."

She was paying attention to her phone and then looked over at me. "Don't stress yourself out or my baby cousin. Ro is a good one, one of the last I think. You should talk to him about it and see what he says. I'm sure he wasn't ready to talk about it right then and there... it's been a few days, as you say, so see what he says now."

"I will." I leaned back on the chair and rubbed my stomach. Yasmine hadn't been too active today and I was trying not to worry too much.

Kiss jumped to her feet when a text message came through her phone. "I gotta run to the store real quick," she lied. I knew damn well that she wasn't heading to no damn store.

"Kiss, you don't need to lie to me about where you're going."

"I really am going to the store. Someone saw some bitch

jump out the front seat of his truck and I'm going to check that bitch." She was already heading to the front and slipping her feet into her shoes.

"Kiss, are you really going to be out there fighting? You're a mother and everyone knows you're with Reese."

"Says the woman mad about an old ex that her man didn't tell her about. You handle things your way, and I'll do mine my way. I don't care if this bitch is a friend, he should have told me about her like Ro should have told you about Lavern," she snapped before grabbing her keys and heading out of the door. I sighed and laid my head back on the couch because she was right. Who was I to tell her what to do when it came to her man? I was over here having heart pains because I didn't know what my man was up to and why he chose to lie to me about things he didn't have to lie about. Before going to lay down, I went to check on Zamari and then went to take a nap.

"Baby you been sleep all day? You good?" I felt Priest gently shake me from my sleep. Squinting my eyes, I closed them back because he had the bedroom light on.

"Turn the light off please," I whispered and pulled the covers closer to my face. I didn't know how long I had slept, but the sleep I had was well needed. It put my anxiety at rest, and I felt well rested. "What time is it?"

"Ten at night. I just came in an hour ago. Love said you've been sleeping since they got in from school. "You alright?"

"Yes, I'm fine," I replied, being short.

Although my sleep was peaceful, I couldn't help but to think about Lavern and Priest's past. I kept wondering why he didn't tell me about her and why he chose to keep it a secret from me. This should have been the last thing on my mind, yet it was what kept resurfacing in my thoughts.

"Babe, what's wrong? You've been off these past few days... Tell me what's up," he demanded.

"I could say the same thing about you." I sat up and slipped my feet into my slippers before going into the bathroom. I tried to close the door, but Priest was right on my ass.

"What you mean by that?" he came into the bathroom behind me as I sat down to relieve my bladder.

Priest didn't give a damn about personal space. He always came in the bathroom when I was using it and didn't give a damn if I was pissing or shitting. He would brush his teeth like it didn't matter that I was letting out last night's meal.

"I'm using the bathroom," I complained.

"I don't give a damn about that shit." He waved me off. "What do you mean by what you said? How I been acting funny?"

I wiped myself and looked at him. "I don't need to repeat myself. You know how you've been acting, and I don't need to explain to you how you have been acting," I yawned. While I thought I was well rested, my trip to the bathroom proved that I was still very much tired and needed to lay back down.

"I've been working and taking care of shit so I can chill once the baby comes."

"Alright." There was no need to go back and forth about this right now. I was tired and he was never going to admit that he was acting funny.

"Alright?"

"Yes. I said alright. I'm tired and I don't want to wake up to you pressing me about stuff. If you said you're fine, then I'll take it that you're fine," I replied and climbed back in bed.

He sat down on my side of the bed and stared at me before he spoke. "I love you and you know that. If I've been acting a way and you feel that, I'm sorry." He bent over and kissed me on the lips.

"Get some sleep. I'm sure you have to get up early in the morning," I told him and turned over to get comfortable in the bed. There was so much that I wanted to say, yet I said nothing. What was the point? Maybe I was tripping and overreacting.

Either way, the heaviness of my eyes caused my mind to go blank so I could go back to sleep.

Priest

2009 – Arlington Projects, Staten Island

"WHY YOU EVEN OVER HERE?" I leaned against the paint chipped hall way wall and waited for a response.

Lavern looked up into my eyes with tears threatening to fall. I hated to see my girl hurt, especially when I was the reason she was hurting. I wanted to keep a smile on her face always. She stood there and stared at me as she crossed her arms and bounced her left leg repeatedly.

"Why are you treating me like this? I tried to call and find out information on your sister's funeral and you never called me back. Ro, what is going on?"

"What is going on? You seriously asking me what the fuck is wrong, Vern?" I switched positions on the wall and looked away from her. Those tears had finally fell.

"Why are you treating me like I killed your sister? I hate that you're hurting, baby. If I could switch spots, I would. I loved Sandy too. You don't think I'm hurting too?"

She was right. I was fucked up not to invite her to the funeral. I couldn't deal with shit and I felt like the entire world was falling by the wayside. It was my responsibility to hold these girls down and I felt like it was all too much for me to bear. Then I had a girl who I loved more than life staring into my eyes, begging me to make her feel whole again. It was something I wanted, yet it was something that I couldn't do, even if I wanted to.

"It's not your fault and I know that. I just need space, Vern. Give me that, ight?" Ghost had me pulling long hours to earn my position

and I had just made it home an hour ago. Stacy, the next-door neighbor watched the girls and made sure they were straight by the time I made it home. It helped that she wanted to fuck me, because I didn't have to pay her. All I had to do is give her false hope that we might fuck one day, and she did whatever I wanted.

Lavern hugged me and then stepped back. "I love you. You know that?" she held onto my face as she stared into her eyes. "We'll get through this together, baby, I promise." She kissed me again. "See you in class tomorrow?"

"Nah. I dropped out."

Her eyes bugged out of her head and she stared at me for a brief moment before she opened her mouth to speak. "Dropped out? Ro, your dream is to be a CPA. What do you mean you dropped out?"

"I can't handle business in the streets and school. Something has to go, and school was the easy one to drop."

"What happens if you get shot out there? The streets aren't the right thing when the girls and me need you."

"The girls need food, clothes, and a roof over their head. I'm not worried about me right now. I'm worried about keeping them fed and avoiding ACS from knocking on my door to take them away from me."

She pulled a paper out from her pocket and hit me in the chest with it. "I received this acceptance letter into LSU, and I called and turned them down because we promised we would do this together!" she screamed. "We promised and you're giving up our dreams and hopes for the fucking streets. I can get a job and help with the girls. I can move in and we can make this work. Ro, you guys are all I have," she begged, cried, and pleaded with me.

The girls needed me more than I needed college. My dreams were something I would have to accomplish another time. Right now I needed to focus on the girls and what was best for them. I didn't want to look back and be in this same apartment, but with a college degree. If I looked back and had a house, cars, and put the girls through college without one, that would be worth far more than a degree.

Lavern wanted to finish college more than she wanted to breathe. Her dream was to be a tax attorney. I wanted that for her, so if she had a chance to go to another college, then that was what she should do.

"You obviously applied and didn't think about me, so fuck it... go." I tried to play nonchalant, but it hurt me to the core to say those words to her.

"Huh? My teacher submitted me for the program down there. I told her no and she did it anyway because she said I was the perfect fit. I told you that. I'm not going to go. I want to be with you," she hugged me and sobbed into my stomach.

The apartment door opened, and Stacy peeked her head out with a smile on her face. "Priest, food is ready, and I made your bed, did you laundry. The girls are getting ready for bed too," she advised me. Stacy did all of this without payment or without me asking. All she had to do is keep an eye on the girls until I made it home and she went above and beyond, which I appreciated.

Lavern put her head up and looked at me. "Why is she in your house? Are you fucking her?" Stacy quietly closed the door, not wanting to get involved in our debate.

I knew Lavern wasn't going to leave and better herself. She was going to choose to stay here with me and toss her education out the window. I couldn't sit back and allow her to do it. Years down the line she would resent me for that, and I couldn't have that. I couldn't have the person I love hate me for a decision she made based on me. That was something that couldn't sit on my conscious and I wasn't about to sit and let her toss her life away for me. I wasn't worth it.

"Yeah, we been fucking," I lied.

The look on her face was one I knew I would never forget. The hurt and pain that was etched onto her face told me that I had fucked up royally. She picked up the paper that fell to the ground and hit me with it, then walked backwards as tears fell down her cheeks. I watched as she turned and walked down the hall and then down the staircase. Little did I know, after that day, I would never see or hear from Lavern again.

I laid beside Justice and listened to her soft snores and how she occasionally grabbed her stomach when she positioned herself in the bed. She was beautiful and everything that I had ever wanted in life. I often thought what did I do to end up so lucky? Justice was my world and now that she was carrying my child, she meant that much more to me. Justice was blessing me with my daughter, and I couldn't be more grateful and humbled. I often thought about how God saw fit for me to protect this amazing woman and our daughter. When I came home and saw her face and swollen stomach it lit my world up. It didn't matter how much bullshit I was hit with during the day, her smile and belly could erase all that in five minutes. It was fucked up that I had been thinking about Lavern since I had saw her at the restaurant a few days ago. She wouldn't leave my mind and all of our memories kept popping up in my head. I had spent years burying our past and it was one chance encounter with her that made her the center of my world again.

I leaned over and kissed Justice before I got out of bed and went into the kitchen. Kiss was sitting at the counter feeding Zamari baby food when I came outside of my room. It was eight in the morning, so I was surprised that her ass was even up. Me and Kiss's relationship wasn't on the best terms right now, so I avoided even seeing her when I came in. She offered me a smile as she put some squash into the baby's mouth. I went into the fridge and grabbed some things out to make breakfast for Justice in bed. Last night, I didn't want to argue, and I could tell Justice didn't either, which is why she shut down and went to bed. When I tried to hold her, she made some excuse about being hot and not wanting to be touched. Justice always wanted to be held whenever we went to sleep. To feel her reject my touch last night told me that I needed to get a grip on this shit and stop thinking about Lavern.

"Making Justice breakfast to make up for not telling her about Lavern?" Kiss snickered as I cracked some eggs into the bowl.

"What you talking about?"

"She asked me who Lavern was and I told her. What I'm surprised about is that you didn't tell her about Lavern yourself," she smirked. "What is that you used to preach to me and the girls?" she put her finger to her mouth like she was thinking. "Oh, being honest." She laughed as she spooned the rest of the food into her baby's mouth.

"She asked you about her?" I was damn near in a panic. Justice knew something which is why she said what she had said yesterday. I thought she knew nothing about Lavern, so I was able to act like she was crazy or tripping.

"Yep, and I told her. I didn't think it was a secret or something. Why are you hiding her?" she questioned.

"I'm not hiding her. Just didn't want to talk about her right now."

"I knew she was back in town too."

"And you didn't think to tell me."

She shook her head. "I don't have to tell you everything. Plus, I didn't think you needed to know since you moved on with Justice."

"Yeah, well I could tell us running into her is bothering Justice."

"No, what's bothering her is that you're lying instead of being honest about who Lavern is. I expect this from Staten, but you?" she tossed the glass baby food jar into the trash and wiped the remainder off the baby's mouth before she picked him up. "You need to assure her that she has nothing to worry about. Right now, I feel like she has everything to worry about," she continued and left to head back upstairs.

I stopped whipping the eggs and leaned against the counter. When I came up with the idea to have dinner with

Justice at our favorite spot, I had no clue that Lavern would be there, more or less working there too. I was caught off guard and knew I should have been honest with her from the beginning. Lavern was someone I spent years trying to forget and act like she never existed. She was the reason I never got into a relationship until Justice came along. She was my first in everything. We were supposed to be married with some kids and enjoying life. Life didn't go as expected and I had to step up to the plate once my sister's sickness got worse. She understood and was there still, but I couldn't ask her to sacrifice her life for me. I did what I did because of my nieces, I couldn't ask her to give her life and dreams up for me. Lavern didn't understand my distant behavior when I lost my sister. Well, she understood, but really didn't get why I kept blowing her off.

When I dropped out of college, she showed up to our apartment and begged me not to turn to the streets. How could I not? College wasn't going to keep the lights on or food in the girl's mouths. It was something that I had to do, and I didn't need her staring into my eyes with those pretty doe shaped eyes she possessed. Lavern had goals and to complete college was one of them. She wanted to be a tax attorney and I didn't want my life to be the reason she didn't accomplish her goals. The day she looked into my eyes and I lied and told her I fucked Stacy was the second hardest day in my life. The look of hurt that was in her eyes made me want to cry. It didn't make it any better that Stacy was waiting in the apartment when I came back from breaking Lavern's heart. I took my frustrations out on her pussy and she enjoyed it, meanwhile I was envisioning Lavern. I often thought and wondered why God chose this path for me? Why did I have to go through so much pain and hurt? It was then when I met Justice that I knew that he took me through all of this just so I could meet a woman like her.

I didn't mean to lie to Justice about Lavern. Yeah, I should have been honest and told her the truth about who she was. A nigga was caught off guard about seeing her. Never did I expect to see her serving us food at me and Justice's favorite restaurant. Since I had ran into her, I had been thinking about if I should reach out to her. I had no clue where to start. Her old number probably wasn't the same and I had no clue where to look. Lavern was a foster kid and had been bounced around until eventually she aged out and went to live with her father's sister. I remember the aunt used to live in West Brighton.

"Why didn't you wake me?" Justice asked as she yawned and went into the fridge. I watched as she pulled out the bottle of orange juice and placed it on the counter. "You okay?"

"Lavern is my ex-girlfriend," I blurted.

She stood there with her back turned before she turned to face me. "Why did you lie about it?"

I shrugged. "Shit, I don't know. The last person I thought I would see was Lavern." I sighed. "You didn't deserve to be lied to and I've always kept it real with you, and I want to keep doing that. You have nothing to worry about when it comes to Lavern."

"Are you sure? Kiss told me how much she meant to you. If I need to ste—"

"Yo, you hear yourself? You don't need to go anywhere. What me and Lavern had happened years ago when we were younger. I'm sure she has moved on like I have." I walked over and wrapped my arms around her waist.

Justice laid her head on my shoulder and let out a sigh of relief. I was pissed that this had been weighing on her mind and I hadn't done anything to put her mind at ease. She didn't deserve to sit here and worry about if me and an old girlfriend would rekindle what we used to have.

"I think you should meet up and talk with her. It's clear that you both have unresolved feelings with each other. With her being back in town, I don't want anything to get in-between what we're trying to do."

This was why I loved Justice. Even though she was worried about Lavern, here she was pushing me to go and talk to the very woman that she was losing sleep and worried about. "Nah, I don't need to do that babe."

She moved back and looked up into my eyes. "Yes. I don't need you thinking and wondering why that woman is back after she left. Go and talk to her and let her know that you're with someone and we're about to have a baby. You need closure and it seems like neither of you got that." She walked over and poured some orange juice and then walked back to the room. Before entering the room, she stopped. "I don't want breakfast, I'm not hungry." She closed the bedroom door and I stood there puzzled on my next steps.

Justice wanted me to go and talk to Lavern, yet I could tell this whole situation was bothering her. I finished making breakfast and then sat it in the microwave in case she grew hungry later on. I checked my messages and then went to shower so I could go meet up with Ghost and Staten at the barbershop. When I finished with my shower, Justice was on her laptop sitting in the middle of our bed rubbing her stomach. She sang lowly to the music that was coming from her laptop.

"I love you, baby," I told her as I pulled some clothes out of the dresser.

"Love you too," she smiled and continued to sing along while rubbing her stomach. Part of me felt guilty for trying to reach out to Lavern, even though Justice had gave me her blessing. I knew it was something that I needed to do. We never had closure and it was well needed for the both of us to square away before trying to continue with our own lives. I thought all my feelings for her had faded away, but they came floating back and the memories we shared were swirling around my mind.

After I finished getting dressed, I kissed Justice and headed out of the door. I knew she was worried and didn't know what would come of my meeting with Lavern. Even though Justice had gave me the blessing to meet with her, I was still undecided about if I wanted to even open that door and open up any skeletons that may come out. It was something that I had to think about. Right now, I was focused on getting to the barbershop to chop it up with my niggas.

TARGEE STREET, Staten Island

"ABOUT DAMN TIME you showed the fuck up. The fuck, you get lost?" Staten said as he was getting his face trimmed up.

Ghost was sitting in the barber chair flipping through a medical magazine unbothered. "My bad. I stopped to get me some coffee. I'm tired as fuck and couldn't sleep," I explained and sat down in the plush chair.

The barbershop was empty. We always came early before the shop opened to get our haircuts and face trimmed up. "What has you not sleeping? Everything seems perfect in your life right now," Ghost looked up from the magazine he was reading.

"I ran into Lavern the other day," I announced.

Staten stared at me and shook his head. "Nigga, why you making shit up?"

"I'm dead ass. She work in *South Fin*," I explained.

"You mean to tell me she didn't become the lawyer she was always talking about becoming?" Ghost raised his eyebrow and stared at me.

"I don't know. I was too caught up in seeing her that I didn't ask her anything. Me and Justice were out to dinner when she came over to our table to serve us."

"Ah shit, did Justice flip out?" Staten asked.

"Nah."

"She know who Lavern is and how much she meant to you? Lavern was like how Freedom was to me. You were hurt when you had to break that girl's heart. Justice knows?"

I sighed and took a sip from my coffee. There was too much shit that I had to do, and this coffee had to do something for me to wake up some. All night I tossed and turned with how Justice went to bed last night. Her attitude had me worried like she knew something and turns out that she did.

"At first, I didn't tell her. I told her that she was a friend." Ghost shook his head. "Then Kiss told her who Lavern was and what she meant to me."

"I'm surprised Kiss remembers her. The girls were young when you and her broke up. Kids usually don't remember people."

"Well, Kiss is fucking nosey, so you know she remember," Staten snickered. "On the real, you need to tell her who she is. Don't let that shit only come from Kiss. Tell her yourself."

"She knows and I did. She told me she wants me to meet up with her and have closure."

"Closure? Free would have went upside my fucking head if I tried to go and have some closure."

"That's what makes them different. Liberty would have kicked my ass for even greeting the bitch," Staten laughed. "I see where Justice is coming from though. Still, she may be opening up a can of worms she may not be able to close."

"I can control myself. What me and Lavern had was years ago. Honestly... I just want to link with her and see where life lead her."

"Uh huh. Tell that shit to a nigga that's gonna believe it."

"I'm dead serious though. What me and Justice has means everything to me. I'm not trying to fuck that up."

"Meet up with her, get your closure and then act like she's still wherever the hell she was at. You can't be friends with her so don't even think about doing it."

"Why not? Me and Chanel are friends," Staten protested.

"Look at the shit show y'all got going on? Chanel pregnant and trying to break you and Liberty up at any cost," Ghost made sure to point out.

"Nah, Chanel knows that me and her will never be together. She be doing too much and I'm not even feeling her vibe lately. She just need to drop my baby, so I don't got to see her ass often."

"You gonna see her ass more once she have the baby. Chanel not about to let you take the baby without her being there. She already be under your ass and she only pregnant," I laughed.

Staten remained quiet and then spoke. "I can't even argue that because she would do something like that." He finished with his line up and I got into the chair. "All I'm saying is that you need to just be careful about meeting up with Lavern. You wanted to marry that woman and give her your babies, so as much as Justice is trying to be strong and allow you to get the closure, you need to be careful not to get closure and end up hurting Justice."

"Yeah, I hear you."

"What's good with you and Lib? I haven't seen her by the crib lately, she good?"

Staten shook his head. "I don't know what's up with her. We been arguing and shit, so I've been giving her space and shit. I know how she hates when people are in her space."

"She not back on drugs again, is she?"

"Nah. I do a little sweep of her house when she's at work, so I know she not back on that. I think the whole Chanel thing is bothering her, so she keeps her distance."

"Everyone around Staten Island is talking about this damn baby shower," Ghost mentioned. "I think she doing too much when it comes to drawing unnecessary attention to you and her."

"I agree." I nodded in agreement with Ghost.

"You have to understand that you're in charge. You're not supposed to be mingling or in the same room as some of these hood niggas in Stapleton, yet she has invited the whole damn hood to this baby shower. I advise you not to go."

"It's my baby shower, how you think that's gonna make me look?" Staten blurted.

"Since when you gave a fuck about how something would make you look? When I was in charge, you think there weren't parties that I didn't want to hit up? I couldn't because of who I was. Niggas will try and get at you because you're relaxed and at your baby shower. Things are quiet, but you gotta remember that shit won't always be fucking quiet when a nigga sees you're doing better than him," Ghost schooled his little brother.

I could tell that Staten wasn't feeling what he was saying, but because it was his brother and he knew he had his best interest at heart, he was going to listen. "Have Mama Rae and Mirror throw a small one with just family," I suggested.

"Yeah, I might just do that." I could tell he was deep in thought about what Ghost had told him. In my opinion, Chanel was throwing this elaborate baby shower just so she could show off and gloat in the fact that she was Staten's baby mama. With all that Chanel was doing, I wasn't surprised that Liberty was keeping her distance, because I would too if I was her.

I finished getting my hair shaped up and kicked it with Ghost and Staten for a while before I went to handle business. The thought of reaching out to Lavern was still in the back of my mind. Right now, I needed to focus on handling business and getting back to my pregnant girlfriend.

4

Ghost

You don't have faith in the ground, you just know when you put your feet on it it's gonna stay solid – Nipsey Hussle

"I don't want to hear shit that you're telling me," I stood up and paced the doctor's office. Today was one of those days that I was glad Freedom had a meeting this morning.

"Mr. Davis, colon cancer is very dangerous and you're at stage two. The change in your bowel movements, recent weight loss and the abdomen pain you've been experiencing is because of the cancer. I'm glad you came when you did," my doctor tried to talk me down.

About a month ago, I was feeling all weird and shit. I couldn't take a shit to save my life and when I did, it was always blood in my shit. My stomach always got these wild ass pains that would take me out and I was losing weight. My appetite changed and I didn't want to hardly eat. I knew something was wrong, so I made an appointment at my doctor to check and see if everything was good. That was two weeks ago, and I had been avoiding coming in for the results. When my doctor called the house phone instead of my cell, I knew I needed to just come in and see what his ass wanted. I never expected that he was going to tell me that I had cancer. I couldn't have fucking cancer. My kids and woman needed me. Shit, my mom, sister, and brothers needed me too. How could I have cancer? I didn't smoke cigarettes and I tried to eat as healthy as possible.

"This shit came at a bad time, Man. I got a lot of shit going on right now with my family. How the fuck am I supposed to walk in there and tell them that I have cancer?"

"Gyson, I've been your doctor for a few years now. I know how much you have going on and I understand this will be hard to tell your family, but you have to. I want to start treatment right away. Before surgery, I want to do five weeks of radiation and then some chemo. After that, I want to run some scans to see if the radiation and chemo will shrink the tumors, so when we do surgery it will be easier to remove."

I heard everything he had said and explained. Still, I was standing here thinking how the fuck I ended up with this short end of the stick? My baby had a rare heart disease and now I had been diagnosed with stage two colon cancer. God had a way of putting us through things to prove that we were strong, but right now I felt weak. How could I be everything that my family needed? Freedom needed me and our kids needed me too.

"Gyson?" My doctor pulled me from my thoughts. "I want to start next week. I'll give you the week to let your family know and then we'll start fresh next week."

"Bet," was all I could manage to say.

"You'll be very sick. I'm not going to lie and tell you the road to fighting and beating this cancer is easy because it's not. You will need the strength of your family to hold you up."

"I hear you."

"I'm going to prescribe you some pain relivers for the abdomen pain and some stool softeners for the constipation," he said as he scribbled on the prescription pad and handed it to me.

"Thanks Doc," I said and headed toward the door.

"Gyson?"

"Yeah."

"Tell your family. Don't wait because you never know with colon cancer. I have lost patients from this cancer and I want you to have the support of your family."

"I got you," I lied and walked out of the office.

I hit the locks to my Rolls Royce and jumped inside. Tears streamed down my eyes as I looked into the rearview mirror. How the fuck did I end up with this shit? I thought losing Summer was going to be the last of my bad days, now this. First it was our son's heart and now my colon cancer.

"What are you trying to tell me? Why are you putting me through all of this?" I questioned out loud.

I knew I wasn't going to receive an answer, still I wanted one more than anyone knew. I needed to know why I was being put through all these tests. I've always been the type to carry everyone on my back, no matter who you were. Since I was younger, I knew I had to step up and be the man of the house. Right now, I wanted to climb in my mother's arm like a little boy and hear her tell me everything was going to be alright. Wiping my eyes, I started the car and pulled out the parking spot. This shit was hard to have sitting on my mental. Free would know something was up the moment I walked through the door. Instead of going home, I ended up at my mama's house. My mama could take a secret to the grave with her. It was why I wasn't shocked that she knew about the twins before I did.

I spotted Mirror's car when I pulled into the driveway. Killing the engine, I climbed out the car and headed to the front. Like always, the front door was unlocked. My mother thought because she lived in a good neighborhood she could just leave her door unlocked. I had a talk about it many times and she still did it. When I entered the house, I could smell the beautiful aroma of food being cooked. My mother didn't work, and cooking was her world. Even though none of us lived at home anymore, she still cooked big meals like we all still lived there. It was the main reason the kids loved visiting their grandmother. It was also why Staten's ass was never hungry. He would always stop by for some food before getting back in the streets. The nigga had two women and still couldn't get a home cooked meal from either of them.

"Gyson, what are you doing here?" my mother peeked around the corner with a wooden spatula in her hand.

I walked over and hugged her before kissing her on the forehead. "I can't come to kick it with my favorite lady?"

"Uh huh. You kids come over here to eat and vent... what's going on now?" she pursed her lips and went to finish cooking.

"I'm good, mama. I really came to check on you," I lied.

"Gyson, I pushed you right out and raised you myself. You don't think I can tell when something is wrong with my son? I don't care how grown you are, you're still my baby and a mother knows when something is wrong." She waved that spatula at me as she stared into what seemed like my soul.

"Mama, I'm about to head out," Mirror came jogging down the steps in some tight ass shorts, sports bra, and sneakers. Her hair was pulled out of her face and she looked different. After hearing that I had cancer, it was like I was seeing things through a fresh pair of eyes. My baby sister wasn't a baby anymore.

"Be careful out there baby. Thank you for coming to check in on me," my mother kissed Mirror, and then Mirror turned her attention to me.

"Hey bro, haven't seen you in a while," she hugged and kissed me on the cheek. "You alright?"

"I'm good. What you been getting into? I haven't seen you in a minute."

"Working out and trying to keep busy. I'm good and I've been being good," she smirked. "I feel like I haven't seen you in forever," she hugged me again.

"Yeah, we need to stop letting time go by without seeing each other. All of us need to stop doing that," I looked at my mother too.

"Neither of you come to Sunday dinner anymore. So, don't look at me, you need to talk to your siblings." She chuckled and turned her back to continue cooking.

"I'm here if you need to talk, Gyson. Just because I'm your baby sister doesn't mean I don't understand things." She lightly touched my shoulder.

"I hear you, knuckle head. You better be out there behaving. I don't want to hear nothing you involved in."

"Whatever, I'm grown. But, I'm good like I said. Ma, I love you and I'll pick you up next week for our mani and pedi date," she reminded my mother before she headed out the door.

"That girl is always on the go. I wish she sit still and get her a career or something."

"She could be pregnant and with a no-good nigga, so I'm satisfied with how she living," I replied.

"You're right. Tell me what is going on," she demanded as she put a bowl of her homemade chicken soup in front of me.

My mother made the best soups. All she had to do was put some stuff into a pot and it always created some magic that she served to us. Since I was little my mother could make a six-course meal out of six dollars. Growing up, we were never starving. I think mothers, especially black mothers had this magic that allowed them to feed their kids no matter what. It didn't matter that she had six dollars and three mouths to feed. It was almost like a challenge for her. She would use that money, whip up a meal and we even had enough to have seconds. My mother was superwoman and I didn't give her enough credit that she deserved for all the things she has done for us.

I took a scoop of the soup and closed my eyes to savor the spices and the party that my taste buds were throwing in my mouth. Pause. "Ma, I don't want to talk about it."

"We're gonna talk about it. Gyson, you walked in here like you lost your best friend. Tell me what is going on, now!" she raised her voice and slammed her hand on the table.

"I have stage two colon cancer," I continued to eat soup like I hadn't dropped a bomb on my mother that could alter her life.

When I finally looked up, she was staring at me with tears in her eyes. Her hand went to her mouth and she tried to form some words, yet she couldn't. Each time she tried to speak, she stopped and thought some more before trying to put some more words together. I sat there and watched my mother break down and cover her face. She was trying to be so strong. I watched her try and be strong like she had been for me as a child.

"I can't imagine my life without you being here, baby boy," she sobbed. "I just can't lose you too," she continued.

I stood up and leaned down and allowed her to break down in my arms. "I love you mama and I'm gonna beat this. I have too much to live for and you guys need me."

"Colon cancer? How? Why? God, why?" she continued to break down in my arms. My mother was always so strong, and could stand strong even when everyone around her was breaking down.

"Ma, I need you to be strong for me. I need someone to be the strong one because I don't think I can be that right now."

"It's so hard," she sniffled. "You're my first baby. I remember when I got pregnant with you." She continued to sob.

"I know, mama."

"I touched and rubbed my stomach like I was further along than the six weeks they told me. I always spoke life into you and knew you would do great things. You were a leader."

"Ma, stop this." I walked away and wiped the tears that fell down my cheeks. "I don't need to hear this right now," I sighed.

"You were a leader. When you and your siblings were younger, you always took charge and lead them the right way. Gyson, you are my angel because you saved me at a time in my life where I felt like I didn't deserve to be here."

"Ma...."

"You're strong and have always proven this. The diagnosis doesn't change that." She wiped her tears and her face grew serious. "Fuck cancer and we're gonna beat that shit's ass... you hear me?" That was the mother that I was used to. One that would never let anything bring her down or cause her to break down.

"Word. I got this."

"You need to tell Freedom. First the baby, now you." I hadn't even told my mother about the baby's heart, but she and Free spoke all the time so I knew she probably had told her. "God is testing your strength. Although we may question his method, we need to go through this test because he has something better on the other side of this, you hear me?" she stood up and walked over to me. "You're going to fight this because you need to be here for your kids." Tears poured down my face as I listened to her speak.

"I hear you, ma," I sniffled.

"Cry. It's alright to cry. You need to let that shit out so that you're ready to fight with all you got. Think of your children when you want to give up. This isn't going to be easy and it's going to break you, but what matters is what you do with those broken pieces after you're broken." She hugged me tightly. "Don't keep this from Freedom. She's your other half and you need to be honest with her, no matter how much this may hurt her."

"Nah," I wiped my tears away. "She don't need this type of stress on her. Any stress bothers the baby's heart. Trust me mama, I'll tell her when I'm ready."

She sighed and sat back down. "As much as I hate that she is not going to know, I understand your reasons. What about your brothers?" I loved how my mother considered Priest as one of her children.

"I don't want to tell them right now. They got their own shit going on and I don't need everyone worried about me."

"We love you, that's why we're worried. You're battling something that is important and that you could die from, Gyson. Don't wait until it is too late to tell them."

"I'll tell everyone when I'm ready," I told her. "I start radiation next week and then I have to do chemo."

"Dammit." It was like it was hitting her all over again and she started to cry. "You're going to be weak; how do you explain that to Free?"

"I don't know. I'll think of something."

"I'll drive you and sit with you. You need someone there to support you. I don't want to hear what you don't need, because I'm gonna be there." She cut me off before I could even speak and tell her she didn't have to.

"I appreciate it, mama," I told her. While she went to the stove, I sat down and started to eat my soup and she snatched it from me. "What in th—"

"Eat this apple," she told me. "You're going to be on a raw vegan diet. I heard that helps a lot. I'm gonna do some shopping for your house tomorrow."

"Ma, give me the damn soup back." I laughed.

"Nope," she told me, dumped it into the sink, and then turned the garbage disposal on. "You need to be at your best. I don't want to hear another word." She held her hand up.

"The hell am I supposed to eat?"

She was in the fridge picking stuff out of it. "I have some veggies so I'm gonna make you some. No meat or any of that sugar mess either," she made sure to tell me.

I've always watched shows and saw how people with cancer lost their appetite, so this diet she was trying to put me on was going to be a breeze if I didn't have the urge to eat.

I hung out with my mama for a few hours before Freedom hit me up asking when I was going to be home. It was going to be hard facing her knowing that I was hiding this from her. Either way, I couldn't take that risk and have her breaking down. Especially with our son in her stomach. I needed the both of them to be as healthy as can be before she gave birth. If that meant withholding information then I was going to do what needed to be done to make sure both she and my son were good. I couldn't lose another kid. Man, I don't think I would be able to go on if I lost another child. It was already hard trying to move on without Summer. I missed her every day. When Rain ran down the hall toward me in the morning, it was a reminder that Summer wasn't here and would never walk down the hall to me again. I kissed my mother and headed out the door. Before pulling out of her driveway, I sat there for a minute.

"Summer, please guard daddy. I know you up there looking out, keep looking out for your daddy," I looked up and said.

I knew she was watching the family and making sure that we were good. As much shit as Shakira did, I prayed she was up there holding our baby girl down better than she did when she was here on earth. After sitting there for a minute, I pulled out the driveway and headed home to my family. Right now, I could use a hug from my kids, kiss from Freedom, and that feeling that everything was going to be alright. I had no clue when I was going to tell Priest or Staten, but right now I didn't want to think about telling everyone. All I wanted was some love from my family and sleep.

ME AND FREE had another appointment with her OB/GYN. She did her usual scans to make sure the baby was doing well. After, she told us to come to her office so we could discuss the birth plans. As far as we knew, we were going to Boston to have the baby. I had my realtor find us some rentals to rent while we're there. I didn't want to be in a hotel where Free wouldn't feel comfortable. With all that we would be going through, I wanted to be sure that we were comfortable. Free was twiddling with her fingers so I took her hand and kissed it. She offered me a weak smile and then looked at the doctor while squeezing my hand.

"So, my colleague, he has decided it would be best to have the baby here. New York Presbyterian Hospital-New York Weill Cornell Medical center is the best in the city. He's already contacted the hospital and has got privileges to do surgery on the baby. We thought it would be best to keep the baby close to home."

I blew out a sigh of relief. "I'm glad. I think it's best for us to keep her here. We'll be surrounded by family and the support that we need," I responded.

"Exactly. It's the best solution that we came up with. However, I want you to keep taking it easy and still come in for these appointments. Monitoring the baby is very important and allows us to know if his heart is getting weaker or stronger."

"Okay," was all Free said. She hated talking about this because it made her emotional. I rubbed her thigh and smiled at the doctor. I was glad that we would be able to stay in New York. I had a few condos in the city that I used for Air BnB, so I was going to pull one off the site and stay there with Free while the baby was in the hospital. Both our mothers were going to make sure the kids were taken care of too, so we were good.

"Also, I want to induce you early next month. The sooner we get the baby out and repair his heart, the better. When I do the scans, he's growing more and more. Take a deep breath, mama," the doctor advised Freedom. It looked like she was holding her breath or something.

"I'm trying to wrap my head around all of this. I'm so scared and feel like I have a ticking time bomb in my stomach. I'm scared to do anything because of the baby and his condition."

"I know and I wish this wasn't our reality. However, we have to do the best thing for the baby and be sure that he's alright and has a fighting chance at life... okay?"

"Yeah," she replied.

"I want her to take it easy. Off her feet as much as possible because I see her feet are very swollen. The last thing we need is for her to develop preeclampsia. So limit her salt intake and be sure to make sure she's elevating her feet, drinking lots of water and not stressing," the doctor advised.

"I got you. I'll make sure she's doing what needs to be done," I promised the doctor. How could I tell Free what was going on with me? She had all of this going on with her and I couldn't sit here and add more shit on top of that. At first, I was feeling guilty for keeping this from her, but now hearing everything the doctor said, I was confident in my decision to keep the cancer a secret.

I held Free's hand and helped her into the car. She sat there with her hand on her stomach staring ahead. She hadn't said a thing since we left out of the office. I was worried about her more than myself.

"You want something to eat, baby?"

"No."

"What's wrong?"

"Are you really asking me this right now? What do you

mean what's wrong? My whole life is falling apart. When is enough going to be enough? I'm tired of feeling like I have to fight through life," she cried. "I'm tired of the shit, G," she continued.

I understood exactly how she felt. It was because I felt the same way about everything happening in our life. When was this going to end? We had been through so much and I didn't think I had any more in me to fight anymore. When was enough going to finally be enough?

I pulled her close to me and kissed her on the forehead. "We're going through a lot right now, but we're going to get through this." I lifted her chin so she could look me in the eyes. "I love you and I know how much we're gonna fight for our child."

"I'm gonna fight, but I'm tired too," she admitted.

Since finding out about our son's heart condition, she forced herself to eat because of the baby and hardly slept. All Free took was cat naps and then she was on her laptop trying to get work done. I tried to push her to hang with her sister or do some shopping, yet all she wanted to do was lay down and try and put everything out of her mind.

"Look on the bright side, we'll have our family near us for support. I'm gonna pull one of my rentals off the website so we can stay there. You're gonna be induced next month and that means we'll be able to see our baby boy. Don't let all the negatives outweigh the positives... ight?"

She nodded her head. "You're right," she agreed.

As much of the negative as we had, we had to focus on the good too. I knew it seemed like everything was coming at us at once, but I had to keep in the back of my mind that it didn't rain forever, and the sun eventually would come out. I just needed to continue praying and being there for my family.

5

Liberty

I sat in the front seat as Staten made his rounds around Staten Island. Usually, I wouldn't be bothered with tagging along, but since I hadn't seen him in a few days, I actually wanted to spend some time with him. We cruised around the hoods of Staten Island bumping old school music and occasionally talking. Every so often he would put his hand on my thigh and lick his lips. Staten was so damn fine, and he made me so wet whenever he gave me that look and slid his tongue across his teeth. Being away from him for a few days gave me the time I needed to miss him. Staten wanted me around him all the time and I couldn't tolerate being smothered. I liked to be away and when I missed him, I would come around and be with my man. The reason I kept my distance was because I didn't want him to find out about me getting high again. It was a secret I was guarding with my life. Even though I relapsed, I was proud that I wasn't getting as high as I used to.

Whenever I needed to just relax, I would do a little and then put it away. I wasn't getting high at work anymore and I wasn't chasing down my dealer to re-up so frequently. If I continued the way I was moving, no one would suspect that I was back getting high and that's where I wanted to keep it. I was stressed about life and needed a pick up once in a blue moon. Was I so wrong for that? Staten pulled up a house and killed the engine. Maliah jogged down the steps of the house and met him half way. I got out the car and she smiled at me and greeted me.

"What's up, Lib? How are you?"

"I'm good... you?"

"Chilling. I see you riding around and getting it with this nigga," she joked and gently shoved Staten's shoulder.

"Yeah, something like that," I replied and followed them into the house. Maliah went into the kitchen and grabbed some waters out the fridge and handed me one, then handed Staten one. "I know you hate that other water, so I brought the kind you like," she told Staten.

"Appreciate it." He opened the water and guzzled it down. Maliah watched him like she was amazed by anything he did. She caught me looking and then turned her focus to something else. "So you think this a good location for this house? I'm trusting your word with opening this trap over here."

"Yeah, it's packed at night and quiet during the day. I think it's best to open this one here. We don't have one anywhere near here and it's needed," he replied. "Todt Hill is quiet, but at night this bitch comes alive."

"Ight, I'm trusting your judgement on this," she responded. "What all do you need to set this up? Let me know so I can get Trac out here to get everything situated for you."

"Everything. I think we need to supply everything and see what we sell out of first. We gotta get out of the place of being comfortable and start making moves that forces us out of our comfort zones, feel me?"

"I hear you."

"I'm putting you in charge of this one. Anything go wrong here, that's your ass... ight?"

"Bet," she replied with a smirk on her face. "You packed yet?"

"Nah, I'm gonna go do that shit today or tomorrow."

"Packed?" I butted into their conversation. "What you mean packed?" I turned and looked at Staten.

Maliah was pissing me off because of the way she was looking at Staten. Then the bitch was acting like what I said to him was any of her business. "I'll talk to you about it in the car," Staten shut me down and went to continue talking to Maliah. "On the real, we need to link once more before going OT."

"I'll be in the car," I snapped and went outside and got into the car. He was pissing me off like I wasn't sitting here. Why couldn't he address the fact that he was going out of town? And, why was I the last person to find out about his sudden trip with Maliah?

Staten came out of the house a few minutes later. I watched as he hugged Maliah and then hopped in the front seat. Maliah waved at me before walking over to her car and speeding out of the driveway. Staten started the car and pulled off as I sat there with my arms folded.

"Yo, what's good with you? What was that storming out about?" he questioned like he didn't already know why I was pissed as fuck. Was it so hard for him to communicate and let me know that he was going out of town? I mean, when the hell was he going to tell me? When he was on the plane heading out?

"Why am I just now finding out about you going out of town?" I turned and stared at him. Staten didn't even look phased by my anger or attitude. "When the fuck were you going to tell me?"

"Lib, you be acting like you hit me up all the time or be over my crib. I don't hear from you for days and then you think you have the right to press me about not telling you something. Come the fuck around more and stop being so distant and then you would know," he barked as he sped onto the highway.

"Because I want my own space I don't deserve to know what you're doing or where you're going? Why is that a problem now? You know I like my space and you said that was fine, now you want to bring it up."

"Hell yeah. I don't even know where you are half the time. You were off last week, and I didn't see or hear from you, did I press you? Nah, I let you rock. Stop wanting shit your way, but when it happens back to you, you want to get an attitude."

"Where are you going?" I ignored his ass. He was deflecting from what the fuck I was talking about. When I was off, he knew I spent time with Chance and caught up on sleep. He acted like he didn't know, and he knew exactly where I was and what I was doing. I needed him to stop being so damn dramatic about shit because he was getting on my nerves.

"I gotta go to Belize to handle some business with Maliah. Her mother wants her to learn more about the business and I need to be the one to teach it to her."

"She likes and wants to fuck you," I blurted.

"Bruh, you wild as fuck. Maliah the homie, nothing more. We get this money, talk shit and chill, that's it," he downplayed.

The thing about it, I believed him because that was the vibe he gave off. It wasn't Staten that I didn't trust, it was Maliah's ass. The way she stared into his eyes and did all that play touching, I could tell she liked Staten and probably always did. He was oblivious or acting like he had no clue. However, I knew the look that Maliah was giving him.

"I'm not fucking wild. She was damn near fucking you with

her eyes. How does she know your favorite water? I mean, all the clues are there and you're ignoring it."

"You really comparing the fact that she picked up my favorite water, to her wanting to fuck me? What the fuck be going through your head, huh?"

"I'm just saying, you need to watch her. She wants to fuck you and likes you." I stuck by what I originally said. Maliah wanted to fuck Staten and he was being foolish and believing that she was just the homie. I knew that look and knew that she wanted to do more than just push work with him.

"I'm not watching shit. You're the one that's distant and want to accuse Maliah of trying to fuck."

"Alright, don't believe me. When she in there raping your ass, don't try and come cry to me," I replied.

The car was silent and we both busted out laughing. "Yo, you stupid as shit. Babe, on the real, I'm not thinking about Maliah and shit. All I'm concerned about is getting this money so that I can secure my daughter's future. You thinking too much into it, ma."

"I don't like sharing you and I know that she wants you," I admitted. Seeing how Maliah was basically drooling over him had me jealous as fuck. I wanted to fight her for even thinking she could have my man. Yeah, we argued, and I ghosted him from time to time, but he was still mine and I wasn't ready to give him up. Especially for Maliah's young ass.

"Awe, you getting jealous over daddy? I haven't hit that pussy in a few days, I might need to take you home and hit that."

I blushed and looked away. "You so damn nasty."

"You like it apparently. Bout to press that damn girl cause she gave me water," he snickered, and I rolled my eyes and sat back in the chair.

He did a few drops before Chanel called and asked him to drop off some more money for the baby shower. She was at the salon and the last thing I wanted was to be anywhere near this bitch.

"Why you keep giving her so much money? She just asked for money last week and you handed it to her without no problem," I brought up.

Chanel always had her hands out for money and Staten had no problem giving it to her. It wasn't like she was asking for a couple of dollars; it was always over five thousand dollars and Staten never complained.

"She need to finish paying the people for the shower." He shrugged his shoulders and continued driving.

"I'm annoyed that you keep giving her all this damn money. Does my opinion mean nothing?"

"Honestly?"

"Yes. I want you to be honest with me."

"Nah, it doesn't. Well, at least when it comes to my money. When you become consistent and I don't have to chase you down to spend time with me, then you can have more opinion on what goes on with my bread. I don't be clocking what or who you spend your money on."

I was taken back by his response. "I mean, I guess I get it. I won't speak on your money, child, or baby mother anymore."

"Here we go with this bullshit." He sighed. "You bout to go hide and shit because of what I said." He shook his head.

We pulled up to the salon and Chanel came waddling out the salon. I understood that she was pregnant, but she was dragging the walk. She had her back pushed back and kept walking like her water was five minutes from breaking. Staten got out the car and she reached up and hugged him. All the bitches in the salon were all eyes as she put on a show for them. The tints in Staten's car was so dark that she couldn't tell that I was in there. It wasn't like he was letting it be known that I was in the damn car either. The relationship he shared with Chanel was the reason I stayed away. It was sickening to watch a woman drool over your man, and your man act oblivious to the shit. Staten never put Chanel in her spot, she always did slick shit that she thought was funny.

"I gotta dip but call me and let me know once everything paid."

Chanel licked her plump thick lips, courtesy of pregnancy and looked up at him. "And what about my hair? You not gonna pay for that either?"

Staten went in his wallet and peeled off some money and handed it to her without one complaint. "Here."

"Thank you, Shaliq," she hugged him again and then waddled back into the salon. She put an extra pep in her walk because she knew Staten was gonna make sure she got back into the shop.

When he got back into the car, I damn near lost my eyes because I rolled them so hard. Staten was generous and offered me money, but I never accepted it. I worked and could afford to take care of myself. Being that Chanel had the same job as me, I knew she had the money to get her own hair done. She wanted to use this moment against me whenever we would cross paths. He took her out to lunch a few weeks back and she tossed it in my face each time she saw me.

"Where you wanna go eat? Phillipe's?" he asked like I wanted to be bothered with him. I was done.

"Actually, my supervisor just called me in to work. Can you drop me home so I can change and head to work?"

"You deadass right now?"

"Yeah. I need the money. I'm trying to take Chance to Disney world for his birthday." I replied, lying.

I wanted to take Chance to Disney world, but I didn't have to work. When Chance told me he wanted to go, I started saving for it. It was the reason I worked so hard. Right now, I didn't want to be bothered with Staten and his bullshit. All I wanted to do was to go home, shower and then head to jersey to this strip club I loved to frequent. I stumbled across it one night and I liked the vibe. I was able to sit back, chill and toss money whenever I wanted.

"I can give you the bread. How much you need?"

"I don't want your money. Chance isn't your child, so I'm not forcing you to do for him. Worry about your daughter."

His face screwed up and he let go of the steering wheel. He turned his full attention to me. "The fuck is that supposed to mean?"

"Nothing. It means focus on your daughter and I'll focus on my son," I clarified.

He mumbled something, then pulled off without another word. When I first got out of rehab, I knew for sure Staten was who I wanted to be with. I went right to his house and professed my love for him. It was like after that high faded real life set in and I couldn't deal with it. One minute, I wanted to be all over him and then the next I wanted nothing to do with his ass. Like today, I wanted to be all over him and then that changed quickly. Times like this, I missed Myla's ass. She would be down to drink and chill with me tonight.

When we pulled up to my apartment, I grabbed the door and he gently reached out and grabbed my thigh. "When's the next time I'm going to see you?" he wondered.

I shrugged. "I'm gonna be busy this week, so I guess the weekend."

He looked away and blew air out of his nose. "Why I gotta make appointments to be with my girl? It's like I'm fucking begging to be with you or some shit."

"You always saying this shit. I be busy just like you're busy. Do I be bitching when you're working and can't take me out? Nah, I eat that shit up and let you do you. Yet, you always pressing me and shit about stuff," I snapped.

I understood he wanted to spend time and I wanted to, too. Yet, he acted like I could just quit my job and follow him around and shit. If he gave Chanel that option she would gladly take it, but I wasn't Chanel, and I wanted to have more going for myself other than being known as his girlfriend.

"You right. I'm tripping." He muttered. "Do you."

"I will." I got out the car and walked to my building. He watched until I got inside and then pulled off.

When I got upstairs, I took a shower and grabbed my phone. Part of me wanted to call this other nurse at work to chill with. She was new and from Brooklyn. We took our lunch the same time and she was cool to kick it with. All she was worried about was collecting her money and staying out of drama. When I was about to dial her number, I decided against it and tossed my phone onto the bed. It sucked that both of my sisters were pregnant and couldn't even hang out. That was one thing I refused to do. I wasn't about to have another baby by a nigga. A bitch was tired of being a baby mama. It was time for me to be a girlfriend, fiancée, or even a wife first. With all Staten had going on, I didn't want to be baby mama number two at all. I was content with my son.

I decided to toss on a pair of distressed jean shorts, white tank top, a pair of all white Jordan 1s and I tied an oversized flannel around my waist. I pulled my hair out of the towel and watched how my curly tresses fell down my shoulders. I applied some leave in conditioner and then sprayed some Gucci Guilty on and went out into my living room. Dumping my shit out of my purse, I grabbed my wallet and jeep keys and headed out of the door. I felt so free tonight and wasn't even worried about getting high. I just wanted to drink, have some fun and listen to music. After the day I had with Staten's ass, I just needed a small escape from everything. If I would have stayed with him, we would have ended up arguing at a restaurant. Eventually, I would call him and talk it out. However, I knew right now we both needed some space. I hated that he acted like I was always running away from him or something.

Was it so bad to want my own space? Staten acted like it was so bad to want to be alone. Either way, he needed to get used to the shit.

SMOOCHES GENTLEMAN'S CLUB, **Patterson New Jersey**

I leaned back in my own section with a drink in one hand and a blunt in the other. Some niggas that were having a bachelor's party was to thank for my weed. They had finished up and had a bunch of freshly rolled L's, so they offered me three. I was on my second one with my mind on starting the third one. I took a sip of my rum and coke, and watched the women shake their asses and twirl seductively on the pole. I wasn't into women and I had one experience with a woman and swore I would never go that way again. I couldn't be with a bitch that bleeds just like me. The women strip clubs were much more entertaining than men strip clubs. I didn't want to see no greasy and sweaty nigga swinging around the damn poke shaking his dick at me. Plus, this club was in the cut and there wasn't too much traffic in here.

"Can I get you another drink?" the dark skin waitress asked. She was real cute in a model way. If she was a couple inches taller, she would have been perfect model material.

"Why are niggas stupid?" I blurted.

It had nothing to do with what she asked, but it was a question that I needed to know the answer to.

"Girl don't get me started on men. I hate them right now. A man is the reason I'm working this job and raising three kids alone," she sucked her teeth.

"You have three kids?" I polished off the rest of my drink and handed it to her. Her figure didn't look like she had one kid, and she said three.

"Yep. I have three boys," she smiled and pulled up a picture of three chocolate little boys on the screen. "My hearts."

"They're cute."

"Thanks. I'm about to get off in ten minutes, so if you need anything let me know and I can get it for you."

"I'll take some nachos and another drink," I pulled money out my wallet and tipped her. She accepted the tip with a smile and a thank you, then went to get my order.

I leaned back and finished the blunt and flicked the clip into the ash tray before sparking up the last one. I forgot how good it felt being high off weed. It was a more peaceful and mellow feeling than getting high off coke. Still, it wasn't as strong as a coke high. I lit the blunt, took a few pulls, and bopped my head to the music.

"Damn, I just watched you face like three blunts. You good, ma?"

"And? I didn't think my father was around here watching me," I snapped and continued to puff on my weed. I was so unbothered I didn't bother to look and see who the deep baritone voice belonged to.

"Nah, not trying to be your father or nothing like that." He snickered. I finally looked up and saw a chocolate God staring back at me. His low eyes were red, his pink thick lips looked like they deserved to be sucked on, and he had a low fade with waves. I had to stop staring because I was gonna be dizzy with the way those things were spinning. His smile was majestic. Either he had an award-winning dentist, or he just took really good care of his teeth. They were perfect. I mean, real perfect. All his teeth were aligned, and they were white.

"So, why you clocking how much I'm smoking? You gonna ask how much I had to drink next?"

"Shit, I might. You see, this is my establishment and I don't want to have beautiful intoxicated women running around outside my shit," he chuckled. "Can I sit?"

"It's your place, sit." I shrugged and crossed my legs.

He sat down and waved over the waitress that had served

me. She left the bar and came over to him. He whispered in her ear and she left again. "What's a beautiful queen like you doing sitting here alone?"

I laughed. "You look like the type to call women Queens but be ruining their lives behind closed doors. Save that Queen shit, because I don't need a nigga to boost my confidence and ego." I took a pull and blew smoke out of my mouth.

He laughed and leaned back more in the chair. "Nah, I like you. Who the fuck fucked you over? Your whole demeanor is cold and screams that you don't fuck around."

"Too many niggas who started their conversation off with Queen."

The waitress came over and sat down a bottle of Ace of Spades. I watched as she put the glasses down and stood, waiting to be dismissed. "You're good, love. Kiss the boys for me."

"I will. Love you," she kissed his cheek and headed toward the back of the club. I paid them no mind as I enjoyed my high.

He turned his attention back to me with a smirk across his face. I tried to ignore him, but he continued to stare at me like I had all the answers in the world. "What?" I snapped. "All I did was come out to have a good night *alone*." I made sure to add the alone part loudly.

He was trying to pick up a woman and I wasn't interested in that shit. I had a long and tiring day and the last thing I wanted to do was have a nigga staring up in my face. "You feisty as shit." He waved over another bottle girl. "Get her whatever she want, on the house."

"That's not necessary," I tried to protest, but she had already whipped out her pad and was waiting for me to name anything I wanted from behind that bar. "I'm good, love," I told her, and she walked off quickly.

I pulled money out of my purse and sat it on the table. "I

can cover my own tab. I don't need a nigga covering anything for me." I stood up and headed toward the door.

It seemed like this nigga was going to get on my nerves all damn night just because he owned the spot. A nigga would tell you that they were God if you let them, so who even knew if he owned this spot? He could have just worked here or was a manager. Either way, I wasn't in the mood to have him staring all up in my face like that.

"Ma, I don't want you to leave. I thought you were flirting, but I got my shit wrong. I'm not even that type of nigga, trust." He followed me outside. "I'm bout to head to my other club in Manhattan, so you can stay and chill for the night. Like I said, everything on me," he made sure to add.

I turned around debating if I even wanted to leave. It was a nice night and I didn't want to head home. Being home would just cause me to think about Staten and Chanel's shit. "What type of club is this one?"

He leaned back on the brick wall and lit a cigarette up. "Not a strip club. You heard of *Lighter* in the city?" I did hear about the club. A few of the nurses at work had gone to bond with each other. I turned it down because I didn't hang with those bitches at work, so I wasn't about to hang with them outside of work.

"Yeah, I know a few people who went there," I nonchalantly replied.

"Word. How did they like it?"

I shrugged. "They said it was alright," I lied. Staten Island had barely any clubs. The ones we had were only lit when someone was throwing a birthday party. If you wanted to get lit and party, you had to go to the city or Brooklyn. The nurses that went wouldn't shut up about the place and had made future plans to go there.

"You fronting. You know damn well they didn't say that." He chuckled and took a drag from his cigarette. "I'm bout to dip so go back and chill in the section you were in," he nodded toward the door.

"You real cocky about this club," I had ignored what he had said.

He laughed. "If I know how to do one thing, I know how to run a business. My club is the shit, and I'll brag on it every time it's mentioned."

"Show me that club and let everything be on the house," I tested him. He didn't look fazed by the words that had left my mouth.

"Bet. Follow me there."

"Nah, let me ride with you." It was dangerous as fuck to ride with him in his car. I mean, I had no clue who this nigga was. He could have been a killer or something. Yet, that didn't stop me from following his gesture and getting into the front seat of his black matte Rolls Royce and watching him close the door.

I opened the door. "You good?" he turned around and stared at me.

"Just checking to see if you had some child locks or something on this," I chuckled and closed the door behind myself.

When he got into the driver's seat, he was still laughing at my antics. "Shorty, pussy comes a dime a dozen. I don't need to shoot, kill, or rape for it either. Plus, I'm celibate."

"What hood nigga is celibate? You gay or something like that?"

"Nah. I got out a relationship and I don't want to complicate shit with women by having sex. That shit complicates shit and makes it harder to... never mind, I just don't like fucking random women. Does it make me gay? Nah. Does it make me rare? Hell yeah. Niggas fuck anything with white gel toes now. I'm not that type of nigga."

I could respect everything he had said to me. Men loved to have sex with any and every one that was walking. It was different seeing a man that knew what he wanted and could abstain from sex to get exactly what he was looking for.

"You're rare, that's for sure," I laughed.

"And you are too. I ain't never seen a woman smoke so much weed and have this calm ass vibe about her."

"My vibe is far from calm."

"Other chicks come in there and be doing the fucking most. On Snap Chat or fucking around trying to get the next nigga's attention. You came in there and was on your own vibe."

I blushed. I've always been the quiet sister who did her own thing. I love being alone and while others would never club alone, I was the type to go and sit at the bar and enjoy my own vibe. I don't have time or energy to try too hard for some nigga that would probably break my heart sometime down the line. I did my own thing and if anybody fucked with it, then we could chill. Half the time, women felt like I was trying to push up on their nigga or couldn't understand what it meant to let a nigga chase you.

"I do me."

"I see. Always be you. That vibe you got is one of a kind," he smiled before doing eighty on the highway. "Ty."

"Liberty," I countered.

I pulled my phone out and opened my Insta-Story and recorded the Bayonne bridge as we sped across and threw the EZ Pass toll booth. He had Nipsey Hussle's *Real Big* playing and I stuck my hand out the window and waved it as I rapped along with the song. I was never into social media, however, once in a while I would pull it out and upload something onto it. The speed, air, music, and my high had me feeling on top of the world. I didn't know this man, but in an hour of knowing him, this small gesture had made my entire day.

6

Staten

Found myself, I was lost – Nipsey Hussle

Me and Chanel had watched some chick movie she had been begging me to take her to. Her mother and friends had stood her up, and I was the nigga that ultimately ended up having to suck up any attitude and take her. After the movie, she decided she wanted to eat so I took her to Millers Ale house. I wasn't trying to go to a fancy restaurant. It was one of the million things I loved about Liberty. She never wanted to go to a fancy restaurant. Liberty would rather eat in an Applebee's than have me make reservations for a fancy restaurant. Chanel turned her nose up until she realized I would drop her home without feeding her ass. I sat across from her eating my shrimp scampi. The shit was good as fuck and I wanted them to bring me another bowl of it. Chanel claimed her food was too hot, so she scrolled on her phone and laughed at random videos. I continued to eat until she gasped.

"What happened?" I asked.

"Liberty was out with some nigga. She was in his front seat and everything," she shook her head and continued to study her phone. "Wow, she had a whole little night last night. You allowed that?" she looked over at me.

"What the fuck are you talking about?" I asked and snatched the phone. There I saw her chilling in some nigga's car, then she went to the club and was in a section with a bunch of niggas. She was the only chick. When I zoomed in, I could tell she was fucking high. My jaw tightened and I damn near tossed Chanel's phone back to her.

"Damn, she was out there wilding out like that with another nigga? You two broke up?" Chanel milked it like I knew she would. I could tell everything she saw put a smirk right on her face. This was what I meant with Liberty. She did shit like this, which made it hard to defend our relationship to Chanel. I could only imagine the type of shit that was going through her head as she sat here with a smug look on her face.

"Shut the fuck up, Chanel," I growled and got up from the couch. Liberty had told me she had to fucking work and here she was in the club chilling with a nigga and all his friends. Chanel chatting didn't make the shit better.

"You telling me to shut up like I did something to you. Your bitch is the one smiling up in another man's face.... And she looks high," she shook her head.

I grabbed my keys from the table, tossed some money on the table to cover the food, and nodded for Chanel to follow behind me. By the time she got out of the restaurant, I was already backing out of the parking spot. Chanel waved me down like I was leaving her and ended up tripping and falling off the sidewalk. Putting the car into park, I hopped out and helped her up off the floor. A few white people stopped and asked if she was alright and of course Chanel milked it by having tears in her eyes.

"You good?" I asked as I helped her into the passenger seat.

She sniffled and tears fell down her cheeks. "You so busy worried about this bitch and look what it's doing to our baby? I fell on my stomach, Shaliq!" she hollered.

I wasn't paying attention to how she fell, all I saw was that she was once standing and then she wasn't there anymore, she was lying on the floor. "My bad. I didn't see you fall. Are you good?" I said as I got back into the car and pulled out of the parking lot.

"Take me to the hospital. I want to check and make sure the baby is alright," she insisted, and I sighed.

I cared about my daughter that she was carrying, but at the same time I knew her dramatic ass didn't fall on her stomach. Either way, I knew I wasn't going to get out of taking her to the hospital and waiting for her. Chanel wiped away her tears as she looked out the window and rubbed her stomach.

"I'm sorry." I admit I fucked up and shouldn't have rushed out of the restaurant. However, Chanel was dragging this whole hospital trip. She didn't need to go, but because she saw I was rushing to get to Liberty, she was going to go to the hospital just because.

"Yeah, whatever. You don't see how this bitch's choices messes with my life and now my child's life. Staten, I don't want her around my child at all. You told me she got clean and she looks high in that video. Instead of being with me, who you know is a good woman, with a career and can hold my own, you would rather mess with an unstable woman who doesn't have shit going for herself."

Liberty was stable when she was clean. She had her career, own place and could think for herself. Even when she was high, she was still stable. She managed to hide this addiction for years. If I was never at her house the day her dealer popped by, I probably wouldn't have known she was using. The rest of the ride was quiet as we rode to the hospital. The valet attendant took the keys as we walked up to the labor and delivery department. Since we were close to the south side of the island, we ended up going to a different hospital. Chanel wanted to go to the hospital she was used to, but since she was the same person insisting on going to the hospital, I made sure to go to the one she didn't want to go to.

We were taken to a room where she was hooked up to the fetal heart monitor and the doctors checked her. I sat in the corner on my phone texting Liberty, who wasn't replying. I knew she was either at work or sleep right about now. The doctor on shift entered the room with his charts in his hand. I put my phone away and sat up. We gave him our full attention.

"How are you, mom and dad?" he smiled. "I just came to let you know everything is going well with baby. Your fall didn't do anything to hurt the baby. We're going to discharge you, but I wanted to let you know before they came to discharge you," he explained.

"Thank God," Chanel blew a sigh of relief.

"Yeah, thank you." I knew nothing was wrong with the baby. Chanel wanted to be dramatic and prove a damn point.

"No problem. It's my job. However, during our check, I noticed that you are dilated about two centimeters. Being that you're thirty-seven weeks, I'm a little nervous about discharging you."

"That mean the baby is coming?" I leaned up.

"It doesn't mean the baby is coming right now. Since you have a doctor, I want you to follow up with them as soon as possible. Thirty-seven weeks is considered premature, although all of your baby's organs are fully developed."

Chanel put her hand over her mouth. "What did I do for this to happen?"

"Nothing at all, sweetheart. Things like this happen and sometimes there's no way we can tell what caused it to happen. Right now, you're fine. You don't have any contractions and you haven't dilated any more since you've been here. Make an appointment with your doctor as soon as possible so he can follow your birth plan, if the baby does decide to come." He advised.

My heart was pumping. My baby girl could possibly be coming, and I wasn't prepared. I mean, as far as her room at my house and other shit she needed I was prepared. Mentally, I knew I had a seed coming, but it felt like something that was so far away, so I wasn't prepared for it. Was I good enough to be someone's daddy? This little girl would depend on me for the rest of her life. Was I worthy of something so precious? It was something that I struggled with and fought myself over. I lived a life for just me for so many years. Yeah, Chanel had always been there, but for the most part it was *my* life. Now, I was about to be a father and had to share my life with a small life that would need me for everything. I didn't know how the fuck Ghost lived with this. He had all these damn kids that needed him, and still managed to be a good ass father to them all. Even with the twins, he missed out on so much of their life and still came in and built a bond stronger than ever with them.

I didn't hear what else the doctor said before he left the room. I was so busy trying to get my thoughts together. "When is this trip to Belize again?" Chanel took me from my thoughts.

"Don't worry. I'll be here for my baby," I told her. She wasn't about to make me feel guilty for going to handle business. Work had to be done and I was going to be there to see my little girl enter the world.

"You can take me to my parent's home. I don't want to be alone knowing that I can go into labor any moment and you're out the country."

"I'm not about to argue about this, Chanel," I told her and stood up.

After the hospital discharged her, I dropped her ass to her parent's house and then headed straight to Liberty's crib. I knocked on the door and tried to control the anger that I had been holding in. I heard the peep hole slide open and then the door opened. Liberty stood there in a tank top, shorts and her hair was pulled into a messy bun. She held a bowl in her hand and looked at me strange.

"You didn't tell me you were coming over here."

"Damn. That's how I get greeted now? When do I have to call and let you know I'm coming over?" I pushed past and walked into her apartment. "What you been up to?"

"I just saw you yesterday, Staten." She sucked her teeth.

"You back using that shit again, Liberty?" I couldn't hold it in. Her attitude was pissing me the fuck off. Liberty was acting like I had did something to her or something. All I was guilty of was loving her ass through all the bullshit she had going on, and it seemed like that wasn't enough.

"What in the fuck are you talking about?" she sat her bowl down and placed her hands on her hips. "You barge up in here and have the nerve to ask me that shit."

"I saw that fucking video on Instagram. Who the fuck was those niggas? Why the fuck you look high?" I stared down at her.

"I was fucking high. Is it a crime to smoke some weed? Damn. You be acting like my fucking daddy instead of my nigga."

"I wouldn't have to act like that if you wasn't a fucking crackhead!" I barked and she looked up at me. "You think I want you to be strung out on fucking drugs or going back and forth to rehab? That shit fucking hurts me too, Liberty. You be only thinking about yourself and never about me. I'm in this fucking relationship too, man!"

"You think I want to have an addiction? You think this is the life that I chose? I can't help that I was addicted to coke, I can't fucking help that. I damn sure don't need you pressing me or stalking my fucking social media. Don't you have enough on your plate like your baby shower and annoying ass baby mama? I should be the last thing you're worried about." She sucked her teeth and walked into her bedroom.

I followed behind her as she sat on the edge of her bed. "What do I need to do to fix us, Liberty? What do you need from me?" I begged.

Our relationship was on the rocks and I would give anything for it to be back normal. I'd do anything to get the Liberty that showed up at my door when she was released from rehab. She wanted this, she wanted *us.* Now, I wasn't so sure. Liberty stopped being affectionate and it was like she would rather be alone than chill with me. I don't know the last time that we fucked or even spent time together.

"I think that we need a break. You have a lot going on and I do too."

"Stop with that shit. Besides my daughter, I don't have shit else where I can't be the man you need me to be."

"You can't be the man I need right now. I got to focus on myself and my son. Staten, I don't have enough energy to keep doing whatever this is that we're doing!" she screamed. "Just leave!"

I stood up and headed to the door. Before I walked out, I turned around and faced Liberty. She refused to look up at me. "On the real, I want to be the man you need. I want to be every-thing to you, but I can't do that if you don't want it. Take care, Lib," I said and headed out of the door.

I closed the door behind me and got to my car. Soon as I got in my car, I leaned back in the chair and closed my eyes for a second. My phone buzzed and a text message popped across my screen.

Come see my new crib, I saw a message from Maliah. I sent her a message back and asked for the address and then headed over to her crib.

Great Kills, Staten Island

The drive to Maliah's new crib was something that I needed. I thought about everything that had just happened between me and Liberty. I wanted to call her and tell her that we needed to really sit down and talk but talked myself out of it. From the way she spoke, I could tell this was something she had been thinking on for a minute now. The last thing I wanted was to hold a woman that didn't want to be held. As much as it hurt to end what we had, I knew Lib wasn't the type to be held or forced into something she didn't want to be in. If it was meant to be, then it would come back to me and we would continue to build something beautiful. I pulled up to the gated townhouse community and gave them my name. They buzzed Maliah and she approved my entry. I looked at the three-story stucco town-houses as I found her house number and parked in her drive-way. She stood at the door with a pair of leggings, crop top and fuzzy slippers on her feet.

"Welcome to humble crib," she held the door opened for me. The shined dark oak floors that led down the hall to an open concept kitchen, dining and living room was far from humble. This shit was nice, and I knew it cost Messiah and Rasheed some bread to buy this shit for her.

"Your parents really came through, huh? This nice as shit," I complimented.

She walked to the fridge and grabbed some beers out and popped the tops off them. "Um, I paid for this with my own money. I didn't need my parent's money."

"Stop fronting."

She slid the Corona to me and shook her head. "I know I was raised well and all, but not everything I have is provided by my parents. I think they're pissed that they didn't have a hand in me picking this place out."

"Oh yeah. Why you didn't let them get you this place?"

"I'm grown, Staten. I love my parents, but I don't want them taking care of me. Especially since I make enough money to take care of myself. If I need them, I know they're always there."

"Look at you growing up." I chuckled and finished my beer.

"I've been grown, you just been sleeping," she winked and went into the living room. It was a white couch with black throw pillows all over the couch. She had a black shag rug laying on the floor with a marble coffee table in the middle of the white sectional couch.

"I've been sleeping. Yeah, ight."

"You have. Staten, you know you see me as Messiah's little girl. I hate it, but I know that's how you see me."

"The work you put in forces me to see you as a grown woman," I admitted. "You ready for Belize?"

"Yep. I asked Mariah and she said she'll step in while we're gone. I think my dad had to step in and convince her. Are you ready? Isn't your baby shower soon?"

"Yeah...I want to leave soon after. Chanel could have the baby early and I want to make sure I'm here."

"Of course."

"What's new with you?"

"Same shit. I went on a date the other day."

"Damn, you trying to do it all now, huh? First, your new place and now a date. How'd it go?"

"Horrible. I tried to go with one of Trac's niggas and it was the worst mistake ever."

"Why?"

"He was too fucking dirty. The nigga thought he was going to take me to his crib so we could fuck. I'm so sick of niggas my age. We have nothing in common and I'm tired of having to start our dates off with disclaimers on how they're not going to be fucking me."

"Yeah, I feel you," I nodded my head. "Half of these niggas used to fucking these loose chicks that ain't about nothing.

You... you're different. You bring more to the table than half these niggas."

"I'm sick of going on useless dates and nothing being accomplished. I'm not looking to be married tomorrow, but is it so hard to have someone to pass time with? I don't even have one contender who can just text me. They're all cancelled," she laughed and finished her beer.

"Take your time. Relationships are fucking overrated," I plopped down on the couch and put my feet on the coffee table.

"Says the man in a relationship," she snickered.

"Used to."

"Um, what? What do you mean used to?"

"We broke up earlier," I replied.

"For what?"

"She's not ready to be in a relationship with a man like me... I guess." There was no clear reason why Liberty wanted to take a break. I mean, I knew I was hard on her and could act like her pops once in a blue moon, but that wasn't anything new or a reason to end a relationship.

"Her loss. You're a caring, funny, and good man. Don't let her demons caused you to second guess yourself. She's fighting something that is bigger than you."

"Appreciate it," I pulled my hat down over my eyes. "You coming to the baby shower?"

"Hell nah. I don't even mess around with your baby mama like that. I'll buy you a gift and bring it to your home, but for her? Nah."

"Chanel isn't that bad," I laughed.

"Yeah, you think she's not. That bitch is a bitch and I don't want to have to beat her ass." Maliah stood up and went and grabbed something and came back. "You ate? I can order some food."

"I can eat." I never did get the chance to finish my food that me and Chanel were eating. "What you about to order?"

"Chinese food."

"Get me shrimp fried rice and some braised chicken wings."

"Bet."

I put my foot down and kicked my shoes off and then got comfortable on the couch. Right now, I didn't want to go home and be alone. I wanted to have the company of someone, and since Maliah was here, I would use her company right now. I had to mentally prepare for this expensive baby shower that Chanel wanted to have.

7

Priest

I wanna see you happy, we both come from broken families – Nipsey Hussle

Chanel and Staten's baby shower was expensive as fuck. The food choices weren't like no baby shower I've been to. Chanel had steak, lobster, and all kind of other expensive food choices. If that wasn't enough, the shit had the nerve to be all you could eat. Her parents may have liked to act like they were better than everyone else, but her whole other side of her family were ratchet as hell. Those people took everything but the damn silverware from the baby shower. Chanel glided around the shower with this long dress on while holding her stomach. She thought she was the Queen of the hour and I could tell that Staten was over her dramatics. Still, because he loved her, he stuck by her side and put up with her shenanigans for the entire shower. It was something off about him and I wanted to pull him to the side a few times and ask. It wasn't until Justice questioned where Liberty was that I realized that was probably the reason that Staten had this blank expression on his face.

After Mirror stormed out, Justice was ready to leave so we left too. I didn't plan to stay long because of the way Chanel acted about this baby shower. It was too much heat and I didn't want to get caught slipping. You would think her dumb ass would realize that she's having a baby by the nigga that runs Staten Island, be more low-key, and move smarter. I could tell that was another thing that probably bothered him. Chanel didn't give a damn and did whatever she wanted. We all were there to support Staten and you could tell. Chanel avoided our table and even when she walked by, she did a fake ass wave like she didn't know we were way in the back. From the way the seating chart was, you could tell she put us back here on purpose. It was all about her family. Free had to fake a contraction to get Ghost to calm down. Once Chanel only acknowledged the baby's one grandmother, he was about to go upside her head. The baby shower overall was nice, but it was over the top – just like Chanel.

"You want some breakfast?" Justice asked. I admired her thick body in her silk robe. The sash was tied above her bump as she moved around the kitchen carefully.

"When are you going to learn to sit your ass down and relax?" I laughed and sat next to Love at the kitchen island.

"The girls have to eat before school and I couldn't sleep anyway," she fussed back and placed a glass plate of grits, eggs, bacon, and toast in front of me.

Justice always cooked like this every morning. It was something the girls had gotten spoiled with. One week she was sick, and you would have thought they were going to die because they had to eat pop tarts or cereal. I told Justice she spoiled the girls and she didn't care. Justice came into this house and turned it into a home. The small shit like a million pillows on the bed or comforter sets, I never understood. The matching towel and wash cloths along with the other shit, I didn't get until she came into my life. Her ass made me get a Costco card and we were in there every Saturday filling up on shit that we were running low on. A real woman came into your life and upgraded your shit. It wasn't about the money, because I accepted that she didn't have it when she moved in. Yet, she didn't like the money part get in the way. She came into the house and made a system that caused me to step my game up. I provided the money and she provided the shelter. It didn't matter about the bills and who paid them, they got paid. What mattered was that when I walked through the door, that faint smell of Kiki coconut was in the air, and it felt like home.

"These grits good as fuck," I complimented and continued to eat. Kiss came down the stairs with Zamari on her hip. My nephew was a little heartbreaker with his cute self. His ass was spoiled too and took advantage that we all spoiled his ass. I couldn't believe he was about to be a year old soon.

"Hey baby boy," Justice cooed as she took him from Kiss and sat him in the highchair. She put a bowl of oatmeal in front of him. I never understood why she did that shit. All he did was get that shit all over the place. He got more on the floor than his mouth and caused a bigger mess that she cleaned.

"Babe, you know he about to get that shit all over the floor and shit. I don't want you on the floor cleaning it up."

"He's fine, Ro," Justice waved me off and filled his bottle with some water. "I can get down and clean it up right."

"You shouldn't. You're pregnant and don't need to be on the floor scrubbing the floors because he tossed his food all over them."

"Y'all ready? I have to get my nails done at nine." Kiss sucked her teeth as she grabbed a piece of bacon off Kiki's plate.

"Nails? You gonna come back and pick the baby up and take him too?" I asked.

She laughed. "He will cut up in that salon." I watched as she grabbed her purse.

"And did you ask any one of us to watch him? How you know we didn't have something or somewhere to go?"

Kiss sucked her teeth and slapped her hands at her sides. "Damn, Ro. I didn't think I had to ask you to watch you great nephew. When y'all baby comes, I don't mind watching her," she snapped.

I looked across the room at Justice feeding Zamari. "He's fine. Go get your nails done," Justice told her.

"Thanks, Jus." Kiss went over and hugged her. "I'll be in the car waiting, girls," she told Kiki and Love, then left out the door.

"I know I'm tired of watching him on the weekends," Love sucked her teeth. "I want to enjoy my weekends too," she added.

"Start telling her no. Your nephew isn't your responsibility so stop allowing her to make you feel bad about saying no."

Love kissed me on the cheek. "You know how Kiss is. I appreciate you for listening though," she chuckled and went to kiss Justice before heading out the door. Kiki did the same, leaving me and Justice alone.

Justice avoided looking at me because she knew I was pissed with her. I was tired of her making it easy on Kiss. She decided to have this baby, so she needed to sit down and take care of the baby. I pushed my plate away and wiped my mouth with the napkin while trying to collect my thoughts. She had me so pissed that my first thought was to yell and that wouldn't solve anything right now. Justice was hormonal and would turn this shit around on me and I didn't feel like dealing with it today. It could be any other day, just not this morning.

"Why the hell you keep letting her do whatever she wants like she doesn't have a baby?" I pondered out loud.

Justice wiped the oatmeal from the baby's mouth and then

turned toward me. "She's a teen mom and needs a break once in a while. You're acting like she's running out to go get drunk at a day party or something."

"That's because it's fucking Monday, Justice. You didn't just hear Love complaining?" I emptied my plate and sat it inside the sink.

"I love Zamari, what do you expect me to do? Act like I'm busy so she has to lug him around every damn where?" she raised her voice. Justice hated when I tried to tell her what to do. I could tell from her facial expression and hand on her hip that she was prepared to defend her decision she made this morning.

"And you don't think I don't? I love my nephew, but what the hell is gonna happen when we have our own baby, or did you forget that you're having my baby?"

She shook her head and grabbed Zamari out of the high-chair. "I didn't forget about anything. Maybe you did... you walking around acting all different since you ran into your ex." Lavern seemed to be the subject of conversation these days. It didn't matter what I said or did, she was always the subject of conversation when it came to Justice. I'm not going to lie and act like I hadn't been thinking about her, but it wasn't like I neglected Justice in the process.

"Why do you keep bringing her up?" I sighed. "You are always bringing her up." I leaned against the counter. "What is it that you want to ask? I'm tired of you bringing her up every chance you fucking get."

She left out the kitchen and went into the living room where she sat Zamari in his playpen. She switched the TV on to some cartoons and then came back into the kitchen to start cleaning up. "You've been acting real funny since she stumbled into your life. I just want to know that I'm not wasting my time or you're not regretting what we have."

"How many times I have to tell you that I don't regret shit

when it comes to what we both have? Justice, it's your fucking insecurity that is causing this to make you crazy. Kiss didn't make the shit better opening her damn mouth either."

She swung around so fast I thought she was going to fall. "And why the fuck did she have to tell me? Why didn't it come from your mouth? And, please... stop using the insecurity card. Any woman would feel some type of insecurity if their man's first love popped back up into his life."

"I'm done talking about this shit. You need to stop taking on so much with Kiss. Zamari is her son and she needs to learn sacrifice and realize that she can't pick up and leave whenever she wants."

"She needs help. As much as she gets on my nerves and needs to learn responsibility, she's a single mother because of you, and is scared."

"Wow, we doing that now? You know like I know that nigga needed to fucking go. You forgot all the shit he did before I ended his life?" I reminded her. Justice had me fucked up with what she had just said. "You acting like I fucking knew she was fucking that nigga when I shot him. You don't think I have to look at his face and live with the fact that he'll never know his father because of me?" I barked as spit flew from my mouth. Zamari was standing in the playpen looking at us like we had lost our mind. It killed me how he had the same expressions as his mama. Kiss disagreed, but his ass had her attitude too.

Justice sighed. "I'm sorr—"

"You good. I'm bout to head out," I cut her off. Right now, I didn't want to hear how sorry she was and how she didn't mean it like that.

"Roshon, are you being serious?"

"I'm good," was all I said and went into the bedroom.

Usually, I would kiss her and make it right before leaving the house. Justice crossed the line with the shit she had said. I understood that Kiss was now a single mother and had to figure out this parent shit without a partner for her child. Kiss liked to play that card all too often. She knew everyone had a soft spot for her situation and she played on that shit too much. I never wanted for my niece to be a single mother. Shit, I didn't want her to be a fucking mother. College was always the plan. She was supposed to be heading off to college to do her thing and get a degree. Her biggest problem should have been trying to find the balance between partying and studying. Instead, she had bigger fish to fry with a baby who would depend on her for the rest of his life. Sandy wouldn't have wanted this for her daughter. In a way, I feel like I failed her. I let her down and now Kiss was running around here trying her best to be a mother and a carefree teenager.

"Ro, can we talk?" Justice was sitting on the bed when I came out the shower. I knew she was going to want to sit down and talk. She went too far with what she said, and I wasn't in the mood to talk about it now.

"I'm good right now. I don't want to talk about this shit right now," I told her. From her facial expression I knew she was about to start that crying shit.

Instead of getting deep into why I didn't want to talk about it, I grabbed my clothes and quickly got dressed so I could head out of the door. Justice was going to make sure she got out what she wanted to say, and I didn't want to hear the shit. I understood she wanted to help Kiss and shit, but what would happen when we had our daughter? Was she gonna try and handle two kids at the same time while trying to run her education center? Kiss should have thought about the life she wanted to live before she fucked a nigga and made a baby.

"You're being too hard on her," she decided she was going to speak her peace anyway. "You forget that she's still a teen and needs guidance. That's all I'm trying to do."

"Being too hard? She lives up in this house rent free, no job and drives a new BMW. Her son's expenses are paid for and she parties every weekend leaving her son for you or her sister to watch. How the fuck am I too hard on her? If anything, I've been real relaxed when I should have continued to let her live out on the fucking streets with her seed."

"Throwing up what you do fo—"

I tied my sneakers and stood up. "I'm not discussing what I do with *my* niece. At the end of the day, this *my* crib, *my* niece, and what I choose to do is my choice." I walked toward the door. From her face, I could tell my words hurt. "You're not the only one who can say hurtful shit," I shot over my shoulder and headed out the room. Before leaving, I kissed my nephew on the cheek and then headed out the door.

Justice had me fucked up if she thought I was about to sit here and listen to her ass about my niece. We walked around the crib on egg shells with Kiss and her mood swings. One minute she was good and loved us, then the next we didn't understand what it was like to be a single mother and alone. That shit was getting old and it was fucking with my personal life. For so long I had picked the girls and what they needed over my own. For once, I was choosing to be happy and build a family of my own, and I was tired of getting into it with Justice about Kiss. That shit was starting to fuck with our own relationship, and we didn't need to be in a bad place with a baby on the way.

BERRY HOUSES NYCHA, Staten Island

I killed my engine and hopped out my whip. A few niggas at the corner store stared me down but said nothing. I was comfortable anywhere I went. Niggas didn't want the smoke and I was quick to pull my gun out and get shit handled. Lately, I had been in this fuck it all mood and didn't have the patience for these new age niggas. These little niggas swore they were gangsta but would piss their draws and snitch on their whole team if they were jammed up with the cops. A few of them gave me a head nod as I crossed the street and headed into the building. I took the stairs up to the third floor and found the apartment door I was looking for. Taking a deep breath, I knocked three times and then took a step back. Checking my Rolex, I heard the locks jiggling and then the door creaked as it opened. Lavern stood there with a pair of leggings, white stained T-shirt, and her bare feet. She looked surprised to see me standing at her door.

"Ro, what are you doing here?" she asked and held the door open so I could come inside. Her apartment was nice for it to be in the project. You could tell she took pride in the painted walls, décor, and furniture she picked out. Everything was in earth tones. It smelled like linen and lavender.

"C'mon, you knew it was only a matter of time before I came knocking at your door." I turned and faced her.

She removed her hair out of her face and stared up at me. "The thought crossed my mind, yeah. However, I saw you had a girlfriend and new life, so I wasn't holding my breath."

"Mom, I'm going to play with Lucinda downstairs," a girl who looked to be around nine or ten came out from the back.

"Alright, make sure you're up here for dinner... love you, Rosh." She kissed her on the forehead and watched her walk out the door. "Before you ask, no. She's not your daughter," she waved me to follow her further into the apartment.

"You know, my nigga had this same shit happen to him... you sure?"

"Positive. She's eight years old and I was already gone for a while before I got pregnant with her. Me and her father was married, but we're separated now."

"You got married? What happened to that never getting married shit?" I laughed because as much as Lavern and I were in love, she was adamant about not getting married until she was established in her career.

"I never said I wouldn't get married," she protested. "I said I wouldn't get married until I was secure in my career."

"And how did that go?"

"It went well for a while. Plans are overrated and life never goes as planned," she went into the kitchen. "Want something to drink... eat?"

"Yeah, let me get some Guava juice."

She smiled. "You remembered."

"How could I not? Guava juice is your favorite juice, so I know you have it."

She bashfully smiled as she turned to head into the kitchen. Five minutes later she came back with a glass filled with the green juice. She sat across from me on the other couch and pulled her legs underneath her.

"So...."

"Yeah, how the career go? *South Fin* wasn't in your plans."

She looked down at her pretty ass toes. I didn't have a foot fetish or nothing like that, but I loved a woman with pretty feet. Especially when they got them painted white or some loud ass color. That shit was so sexy to me.

"My soon to be ex-husband is in the army. We moved around a lot after I had Rosh. Every time I tried to enroll back in school, he got orders to go somewhere else. We've been in Virginia for a while before he got orders to come to the army base in Staten Island."

"Army man, huh?"

"I needed to try something new and he was that."

"So why is he your soon to be ex-husband?"

"Before our daughter was born I've been sacrificing and putting him and our daughter first. I've packed up and uprooted my life more times than I would have liked to and never complained. Each time it was time for me to head back to school, it was a problem. He wanted another baby, our daughter needed me, or anything he could find to guilt me with. I'm tired of doing everything for him and nothing for myself." She wiped a tear that fell from her cheek. "My daughter adores her father and is so proud of the man and soldier that he is. She brags about him any chance she gets, and I loved that, but when it comes to me I'm just her mother. I'm the one who is home with snacks or takes her to Target to food shop. I just want my baby to be proud of me."

"And he didn't like that shit?"

"Nope. I was pregnant and knew that it would be impossible to try and go back to school. I miscarried and I wasn't sad about it. I felt like God was giving me a sign to do what I wanted and follow my dreams. He wasn't happy and wanted to try again. His parents were on his ass for baby number two and I just don't want to be a baby machine."

"Damn, I'm sorry to hear that." I shook my head. "How did you end up here and working at *South Fin*?" It was something that I had to know.

"I left him and took our daughter. My aunt died a month before I decided to leave and she left this apartment to my cousin, but she moved to Alabama, so I took it over. I applied at *South Fin* and take classes at the college of Staten Island at night."

"When the fuck you sleep?" I joked to lighten the mood.

"Whenever I can. I'm just trying to gain my independence. Rosh's father isn't a bad man, he was just raised a different way from me. His mother has stayed home while his father provided, so he wants what he was raised on. Still, it's not a life that I want, and I can't believe I allowed myself to get to place where I was depending strictly on a man."

"It's nothing wrong with that, Vern. Don't beat yourself up, that was your husband. We lose our way and that's fine long as we find our way back. You seem like you're finding your way back just fine."

She offered a weak smile and removed her hair from her face. "Your girlfriend is pretty," she complimented.

"Yeah, she's beautiful," I smirked thinking about Justice. It pained me to leave the way I did this morning.

"And a baby too? I'm so happy for you, Ro. How do the girls feel about her?"

"They love her, man. We're all excited for my daughter to get here."

"Oh lawd. Your first baby is a girl. She's gonna have you wrapped around her finger just like the girls," she giggled.

"Word."

"I've missed you," she whispered. I looked up from my watch and our eyes connected. My heart beat sped up as I stared into her brown eyes. "I really have," she added.

She stood up and came and sat on the same couch as me. I grabbed her hands and kissed the top of her hand. "I missed you too. A few times I wanted to hit you up and see if your number was the same."

"I wanted to do the same too," she admitted. "There's not a day that passed that I didn't think about you and the girls."

"Shit was hard at first, but we're good."

"I see," she smirked and dusted off my Balmain jean jacket. "Fresh to death, eh?"

"You know how I do." We both shared a laugh. She was about to speak, and her phone started to ring. "Let me take this," she said and left the room.

I sat there and checked my phone and saw a few missed calls from Justice. If something was wrong one of her sisters would have called me. She just didn't like that I left the house and didn't allow her to make it right. I wasn't ready for her to try and make what she said right. How could you make that shit right? I mean, you could apologize, but what would that do? You already spoke on how you were feeling secretly, so why try to make it right? If that was how she felt, she needed to speak on how she felt.

You good? I sent her a text. Her ass must have been waiting by her phone because she sent one back quickly.

No, I'm not. We need to talk. Since when you leave the house without fixing shit?

Not in the mood to talk about it. We good. That's all that matters

Wow. I think I need to go and stay with my sister for a bit. I can't live with someone who doesn't want to talk things out. We're not fucking kids, Roshon!!!!!!!!!!!!!!!

Do what you need to do.

I can't believe this. Since that bitch came into your life you've been acting really funny. I'm cool on you. Believe that.

You're hormonal

Hormonal? Bet.

Sayless

Less is said!!!!!

I laughed because Justice's ass always had to have the last word. She could never end an argument without having the last word. I put my phone away as Lavern came from the back with her phone in her hand.

"Everything good?"

"Yes and no," she admitted. "Sitting here and talking with you, everything is right. However, my ex is coming to pick me and my daughter up to go shopping for their vacation."

"Oh word? I gotta run some errands anyway," I stood up and she wrapped her arms around my body tightly. "I forgot how soothing your little ass hugs were."

She pulled back and hit me in the chest. "Be quiet," she giggled. "Can we hang out again or..."

"Or what?"

"Your girl would mind? I don't want any issues; I just miss you. We were friends before anything else," she made sure to add.

"Yeah, we can make that happen. Let me take you out to dinner or something when you're free."

"This weekend is good. I work the morning shift so I'll be off, and my daughter will be in Jamaica with her grandparents and father."

"Bet. See you then." I hugged her again and we walked to the door.

She held the door open and stepped out into the hallway. "Thank you for stopping by, Ro. I thought seeing you at the restaurant was enough, but seeing you today just confirmed that I've missed having you in my life."

I pulled her in for one more hug and kissed her forehead. "Word. I'll see you this weekend."

"K," she smiled as she closed the door.

I headed out the building and got back in my car. Before pulling away, I hit my steering wheel and leaned my head back for a minute. Lavern always was the one for me. She was my person and was supposed to be by my side as I built all of this. Still, I couldn't be selfish and had to let her go follow her dreams. It was hard as fuck and that shit hurt every damn day. When you love someone, you put their needs before your own, even if that means that you may end up being the one hurt. My phone buzzed and I looked over at my phone in my passenger seat. Ghost's name came across the screen.

"What's good?" I answered right away.

"Meet me at the address I'm about to text to you," he said.

"Bet," I replied and ended the call. Taking a deep breath, the text message came through like clockwork. Looking at the address, I put it into my GPS and was on my way. I knew I needed to get my emotions in check before I messed up everything I worked so hard to build with Justice.

8

Ghost

I just want your pleasure; you just want my pain – Nipsey Hussle

I sat in the chair with an IV hooked up to my arm receiving chemo therapy. My doctor had decided on doing both at the same time. She had me in and out of this place so much that it was becoming harder and harder to come up with lies to tell Freedom. She was already becoming suspicious and wanted to come with me each time I told her I had to leave out. The chemo was the main thing that took me out. Usually a few days after it would hit me, and I would be weak as shit. I'd be so weak that I couldn't even pick up Rain when she ran for me to pick her up after school.

Hiding that I had cancer was becoming so fucking hard and I was carrying a huge weight on my chest. My mother was the only person who knew, and she kept the secret to herself. It hurt seeing the look of pain on her face each time she looked up into my eyes. She had been the one driving me back and forth to my appointments. After this morning, I knew I had to tell my brothers. This shit was too much on her heart. It was one thing to know, then another to watch me go through this. There was so many side effects to the damn chemo that I found myself vomiting after I ate. My hair hadn't fell out and I was grateful for that shit. It was only a matter of time before that shit happened too.

"Yo, you good?" Priest rushed over soon as the nurse showed him the room. I had my doctor arrange for me to have my own private room when I received treatment.

"Yeah, I'm straight," I lied. For as long as I could remember, I had always been the one with all the answers, always alright and the one who everyone relied on.

Priest was unsure, yet he took a seat across from me. "I saw Staten pull up. That nigga was on the phone barking at somebody."

"Probably Chanel's dumb ass," I chuckled.

Like clockwork, Staten entered the room wearing a mean mug across his face. "Why you in the hospital?" he walked over and dapped me.

"Damn, is that the first thing you both have to say?"

"Hell yeah," they both said in unison.

"You in here with a IV in your arm and you're worried about why we're asking questions... tell us what's up?" Priest leaned forward and gave me all his attention.

"G... you scaring us, man," Staten added.

I sighed and looked out the window. "I have stage two colon cancer," I admitted out loud. It was something I hadn't said out loud since I told my mama. It was funny how shit didn't seem real until you said it out loud. The thoughts always swirled around in my head. Some nights I couldn't sleep because I worried about Free and the kids if something happened to me. Even then, I was able to shut the thoughts off and try and get some sleep. Saying it out loud to Priest and Staten made the shit ten times real.

"Nah, nah, nah, nah," Staten got up and the chair fell to the ground. "I lost my niece and I can't lose my brother too... nah, God can't keep handing me all these L's," his voice cracked as he paced the floor.

Priest sat there with his hand on his chin staring into thin air. I could tell from his facial expression that he was processing everything I had said. Priest and Staten were opposites. While Staten would fly off the handle and be ready to kill any and everybody, Priest sat and thought shit through and allowed his mind to process shit before he flew off the handle. Staten slid onto the floor in front of my legs and cried like a baby. He cried so hard that I held my hand on his back. This was my little brother, world, and first best friend. My brother meant so much to me and I hated to see him hurting like this.

"G, I can't lose you... I just can't. It's not an option. How much money I gotta pay, how much?" he sobbed in my lap.

"Money not the issue, bro. Look at me," I told him, and he stared into my eyes with a tear stained face. "I'm gonna fight this shit. You know me to ever back down from something?" I chuckled, trying to make light of the situation.

"This not a street war, G. You got cancer, nigga. I've seen that shit take out the toughest players," he sniffled.

"Cancer met its match, feel me? I'm not about to let this shit take me out, you heard? I need you to be strong for me, baby boy."

"What is your doctor saying?" Priest finally spoke.

"She's the best of the best. We have a treatment plan and she's hopeful. I'm not fighting her or being stubborn either. I realize that this shit is bigger than me. I gotta be here for my kids and Free, they need me too."

"What do you need me to do? I'm here to do whatever you need."

"Drive me to these appointments. Mama been driving me, and I can tell this shit is tearing her apart."

"Mama didn't tell me shit," Staten chimed in.

"I told her not to." I stretched my arm to avoid getting a cramp. "I wanted to be the one to tell you both myself."

"What about Free?" Priest questioned.

"She doesn't know. The baby's heart condition is endangered if I tell her this right now. I'm going to tell her, just not right now."

"When it rains it fucking pours. I'm cancelling the trip to Belize." Staten got up from the floor and pulled his phone out.

"Nah, you're going. Business must continue. You're the main nigga in charge. Shit doesn't stop because you got personal family shit going on. I'll still be here when you get back, go handle business."

While I was running shit, there was so much that happened to me, but I had to continue to run shit. I couldn't allow shit to stop me from doing my job in the streets. I could tell that Staten was hurting by this news, but he had to toughen up and continue to handle business like he was called to do. Sitting in America and being sad about me wasn't going to do anything except drive him crazy. He needed to stay busy. If Free could travel, I would go away to my villa out there to spend time with her.

"Damn, I can't believe this shit. Why the fuck he keep punishing us?" Priest stood up and leaned against the wall.

"Man, I don't know. All I know is that I'm gonna fight this shit and win. Cancer fucked with the wrong nigga, ight?" They both nodded their heads. "Life continues. I just want someone to drop me off and pick me up. Y'all got lives so if you can't, don't be afraid to tell me that you can't. I can find other ways to get here."

"Nah, I got you. We can split up the days you need to come," Staten stated.

"I appreciate y'all for real. Keep this between us."

"We got you," Priest stood up and dapped my hand. "What was you barking about when you pulled up?"

I could tell he was trying to switch the subject because Staten was about to become emotional again. My brother was tough as shit, but it was his family that would bring him to his knees. The only times I've seen him cry was when it had something to do with his family. Family meant everything to us.

"Chanel little stupid ass. She mad about the baby shower."

"What she mad about?" I asked. The baby shower was a waste of my time. If it was up to me, I would have gone off and ruined the whole thing. Free was the one who held me under control and begged me to behave.

"She got the pictures back and is mad that I'm not smiling in none of them. I can't wait until she has the baby because I'm sick of this emotional shit." He sat back down in the chair to the left of me.

"Dawg, that don't got shit to do with the baby. You just seeing Chanel how we all have seen her for years. She's selfish and it's always been all about her," Priest beat me to the punch.

Chanel has always acted like this, so this was nothing new to any of us. When it came to Staten, it was new to him because he had finally stopped babying and spoiling her ass. "Nah, stop fronting," he protested.

"Chanel is spoiled, and you created that monster. I don't like the fact that she acted like mama was a second thought."

"No offense, G, but you used to do the same shit when you was with Shakira," Priest called me out. I couldn't even front, I did put her first before my mother to keep the peace in our home.

"The difference between what he used to do and me, is that I told her the table to put y'all at. We got into an argument on the way back to her parent's house because of the shit. I know one thing; I'm trying hard not to catch a case."

I laughed. "What Lib got to say about this?"

"Nothing. We broke up."

"Broke up?" Priest hollered.

"Yeah, Soulja Boy, you want the whole hospital to hear?" he snapped. "She said she couldn't do it anymore and we needed to end it."

"Damn. How you feel?"

"Like someone stepped on my fucking heart. Dealing with Chanel was easy knowing I had Liberty in my corner. Now I feel like I'm fucking alone and trying to handle her alone."

"Stop bowing down to her every need. Chanel can't have half of what she does without you. You're the one who started this shit, so you're the one who has to put an end to the shit too," I advised.

"Yeah, I gotta do something because I feel like I'm gonna have a ulcer or some shit with her ass."

"She a nurse so she can fix it for you too," Priest laughed.

"Fuck up." Staten laughed.

"On the real, make it right with Liberty. She probably got tired of having your shit mixed with hers while she's trying to work on being sober."

"She was smoking weed on Insta-Story with some next nigga. I asked her about it, and she came all left and ended the shit. You believe that shit? She broke up with me like I did some shit to her."

"Damn, she was the one to break up with you?" I shook my head. "Who was the nigga?" I wondered out loud. Every nigga knew that Liberty was Staten's girl, so no nigga was crazy enough to step to her.

"I don't know, I ain't never seen him around before. That's not even the problem, I wanna know why she don't think that we'll work. How she just decide to end us without asking what the fuck I want?"

"Liberty playing shit like she the nigga," Priest laughed.

"Word," I agreed. "Lib always been different tho. I think you met your match when it comes to her."

"All I want is to be loved and she being all cold and shit. Got me feeling like a bitch or something. I'm supposed to stop by because she told me to come get my stuff."

"Oh damn, she letting it be known that ain't no coming back from this," Priest was the first to point out.

"Yeah, I guess she is." He sat in deep thought with himself.

"Oh, you have company. I'm glad, I've told you going through this alone is hard mentally and physically," my doctor came into the room.

"Yeah, these are my brothers."

"Hi, brothers," she smiled and examined my bag of fucking poison. "You're just about done," she grabbed some gloves and took the IV out of my arm. She put a band-aid on it and rolled the pole into the corner of the room.

"I already know the rules," I beat her to the punch.

"Make sure he takes it easy and tries to eat. I know your appetite hasn't been much lately, but you need to get some food into your system. Soups and smoothies are the best."

"We'll make sure he's good," Staten promised.

I grabbed my stuff and we made our way to the parking lot. "I'm gonna ride with Priest. We need to ride by the trap anyway." I told Staten.

We hugged and dapped up. "Ight, I gotta stop and do some shit before I head to meet up with Maliah."

"Bet. Be safe." I told him.

"Love you, G... for real." He told me.

"I love you too, bro." I replied and I got into Priest's car.

The car ride was silent as we drove through Staten Island. I could have been treated in Jersey, but Staten Island worked best since I had to come out here anyway. I could tell something was on Priest mind and he didn't want to speak on it or didn't know how to speak on it. He made a left and I decided to break the silence.

"What's good with you?"

"Nothing. Trying to keep up on work and deal with Justice's hormonal ass."

"Lavern got something to do with any of her hormonal changes?" Lavern meant a lot to Priest, so I knew he couldn't go on about life like he hadn't run into her.

"She brings her up anytime we argue, even though the argument is never about her. I told her she has nothing to worry about and she's still tripping and shit."

"You sure she doesn't have anything to worry about?"

"Nah, she don't. Me and Lavern are friends. She acting like me and her gonna get back together or something. Lavern got a whole seed and an almost ex-husband."

"How you know all of that?"

"Cause I was at her crib before you called me and told me to come to the hospital."

I shook my head. "Justice knew?"

"No, but she was the one who told me to talk to her."

"And was that before or after Lavern became the topic of discussion in your house?" Priest was in a tricky place. He loved Justice and Lavern was the woman that he was supposed to spend his life with. I could see where he was torn on what to do about the situation. The one thing I knew was that he and Lavern couldn't be friends. It didn't matter how much time passed, they couldn't be friends because they were once upon a time, the love of each other's lives.

"Before," he admitted.

"Yeah, you need to tell her."

"What's that going to prove? She gonna just be crazy and I don't need her stressing with my baby in her stomach."

"What happens if she finds out without you telling her? You don't think that's gonna stress her out more?"

He was pondering on what I had said to him. "I hear you."

"I hope so. Don't fuck up your home over something that was years ago. Lavern was your past and Justice is your now and future. Unless you're prepared to switch things, you need to stop chasing the past."

"I hear you."

"Yeah, you don't hear shit I'm saying. You gotta make the decision on your own, but don't hurt Justice," I warned him.

"I would die before I do some shit like that. I really do hear you, G... for real."

"Bet," I said, as we pulled up to the trap. Before stepping out, I checked my watch and then went to handle business. I knew I would be heading home late and would have to hear Free complain.

"WHAT TIME DID you get in last night? I tried to wait up for you, but my eyes grew heavy," Free stood at the foot of the bed holding her stomach and one of the four post that held our canopy bed up.

I yawned, stretched, and sat up. "A little after two. I tried to pull away in time to tuck the kids in bed, but you know how this shit goes."

"Yeah... I know how this shit goes," she sighed.

"And what does that mean, babe? Why you acting like you don't know how this goes."

She let go of the bed post and stared me in the eyes. "When you said you were giving everything up to Staten, I expected you to be home more. I saw you more when you were running shit." She complained.

"Baby, I'm trying to help Staten get settled into his position more. I can't just step back and leave him out there to drown," I lied. Staten knew what was expected and did his thing. He had been watching me doing it for a while and hopped into position right away. Even with him running shit, there were certain things that I still stepped in to handle.

"You leave early in the morning and then don't answer your phone half the time. Then, you climb into this bed at late hours and expect that I'm not supposed to question none of this. We're about to have a damn baby and I can't even get in touch with you to talk about something. Like, what the fuck," she vented.

Here I was trying to avoid stressing her out, and my actions along with my absence was doing just that. I got out the bed and closed my eyes briefly because my legs were on fire. I felt like I had ran around the world and then came to take a nap.

"Ma, I don't want you to feel like that. You know you and the kids mean a lot to me and I want to spend all the time with you."

"Hmph, I can't tell... and why are you walking like that?" she noticed how I was walking. "G, is there something you're not telling me? I feel it's something in my spirit or something."

"If it was something that I needed to talk about, I would have spoken to you about it. My knees just been bothering me and shit." I lied. It was a half lie. My knees hadn't been bothering me, but the side effect from the chemo had my knees, legs, and everything else in pain.

"Gyson, I don't want to get in the habit of hiding shit from each other," she whined.

Pulling her close, I kissed her lips. "I love you, Free."

"I love you too, but did you hear me?"

"I heard you tell me that you're about to climb into bed with me and relax. Your ass is up and got my baby stressing about nothing."

"He's fine." She giggled. "I'm not fine, I need to feel you inside me," she moaned and touched my dick. Usually I would be hard as a rock, but nothing was happening. She rubbed around for a minute and then took her hand back. "See, I knew

I wasn't crazy. You're not attractive to me anymore," she accused.

"Free, why you acting crazy and shit?"

"I'm acting crazy. I can just breathe on your neck and your dick would be hard as shit. I'm rubbing and touching it and it's still soft as a baby's ass." She popped her neck from one side to the next.

"You think I want to get hard when I'm in fucking pain?" I lied. "I just told you that I was in pain and you thinking about yourself. I'm going to the bathroom and you can go about your day." I faked like I had an attitude.

I heard her mumbling under her breath, so I slammed and locked the bathroom door before going to the water closet. I stroked my shit a few times and thought about Free bending over and shaking that fat ass of hers. Nothing. I even thought back to the last time she sucked my dick so good I had tears in my eyes. Still. Nothing.

"The fuck is going on?" I whispered to myself. My ass was in this bathroom playing with my dick like a fucking broken rope. I was still very much attracted to Free. The problem wasn't her; it was me.

After tugging at my shit and thinking about all the freaky things we did, I gave up and went to wash my hands. When I came out the bathroom, Free was nowhere to be found. Grabbing my phone, I dialed my doctor's private number. The only way I would be treated by a doctor was if I had their private number. They wasn't about to charge me out the ass and try to refer me to their physician's assistants and nurses. I wanted to call her ass and wake her ass up.

"Gyson, is everything alright?" she sounded alarmed.

I walked into my closet. "Yo, my dick not working. I got my woman in here thinking I'm not attracted to her and shit." I harshly whispered as I paced the floor in my closet.

"Ah, that's a side effect of chemo. Some men lose interest, or their penis fails to work. I should have told you about that, but it rarely happens."

"How long is this shit gonna keep happening?"

"There's no telling. It can get better next week, or weeks after you finish your last treatment. It's not permanent, so don't worry about that."

"How the fu—"

"Why you on the phone whispering in the fucking closet, Gyson!" Free yelled, causing me to damn near jump out of my skin.

I ended the call without saying another word to my doctor. I quickly grabbed a dress shirt and turned around slowly, preparing myself for the tongue lashing she was about to lay on me.

"Why you doing all of this? Since when I can't be on the phone in the closet?"

"Why are you whispering? It's another bitch? I know it's another bitch, I can tell from the way you've been acting," she continued to accuse me of fucking with some mysterious bitch.

"When do I have time to fuck someone else? If I'm not here, I'm working and when I'm not working I'm here... so answer your own question, when do I have time to have another bitch, Freedom?"

"I'm not stupid and I've been having a feeling for a while, but I've kept quiet about them." I put the dress shirt down and left the closet. Free was being crazy and I wasn't about to sit here and listen to her dumb ass theory's on who I'm fucking. "You hear me, Gyson!" she continued.

"You really arguing about shit that doesn't matter when we have to prepare for a baby with a heart condition! Free, check yourself or I'm bout to dip and leave."

She gasped so loud. "You threatening to leave me now," the waterworks started, and I sighed. "I never threatened to leave you and you're just ready to up and leave me?"

"Quit with all that shit, you know I would never leave you and my kids. I just need peace, that's all I'm asking for," I begged as I climbed back into bed.

"Then talk to me. Tell me what is going on with you?"

"I'm missing Summer. I been trying to push forward, but she's always on my mind," I told half the truth. My daughter was always on my mind and I missed her more than anyone knew. At this moment, I needed to get Free off my back. I was five minutes from telling her what was really up, and I knew she couldn't handle that shit right now.

She touched my hand. "I'm sorry."

"It's all good. I don't like to bring you all down about it, so I keep it to myself."

"Talk to me about it. Bottling it all up isn't good for you, babe." She tried to convince me. "I'm gonna make us some breakfast and then we can relax and watch movies."

"Ight." I said and leaned back in my bed. I was happy to get her ass off my back, but frustrated because I had to deal with this cancer shit. If you asked me, Chemo did more bad than the actual damn cancer. While I had some quiet, I closed my eyes and tried to get some sleep before Free's mood swings started up again and I was being accused of buying a damn dog behind her back.

9

Maliah

It's four in the morning, tell me that you want it. Bend you over, I got you moaning. You luh this shit – Nipsey Hussle

Belize

I COULD TELL something was different when it came to Staten. It could have been the fact that he and Liberty were no longer together, or it could have been something else. The entire plane ride was quiet, with him listening to his headphones. I tried not to pry and give him his space. If he wanted to talk, he would have spoken to me about it, right? It was nagging me that I didn't force him to talk about it. The main reason I didn't stick my nose into his business was because I didn't like when someone pried into my business. We had been here two days and it was business per usual. I knew that was the whole point of the trip, still I expected that we would joke, chill, and explore the town together. His mind was everywhere, but here in Belize.

I stepped out of the pool and the housekeeper passed me the towel to dry off with.

"Thank you," I politely thanked her and wrapped the towel around my body. Staten had went to town to do something, so it was just me and the house staff here.

I walked into the kitchen and stood there for a second before looking in the fridge and cabinets. He didn't live here full-time, but from the full stock of food, you could have sworn that someone lived here regularly.

"Can I make you something to eat, madam?" the housekeeper who passed me the towel asked.

"No, I want to cook something for me and Mr. Davis," I replied. "Can you get the pots and things ready, I'll come down when I'm showered."

"Right away, madam."

"Maliah."

"Excuse me, madam?" she looked at me confused.

"My name is Maliah, call me that. I'm too young to be called madam... I should be calling you that," I smiled when she put a smile on her face.

"Okay, ma... Maliah." She finally got it right.

"Oh, and have the guys set up a table on the beach," I ordered and continued up the stairs.

I rinsed the chlorine off my body and out of my hair before stepping out of the shower. Looking through my luggage, I pulled out a white jumpsuit with wide pant legs. My hair was wet and curly, so I added some leave in conditioner and allowed it to hang freely down my back. I spritzed a few drops of my favorite Tom Ford perfume on and then slipped my feet into my tan Hermes flip flops before heading back downstairs to cook.

My mother wasn't the type to sit and teach me how to cook food. She taught me how to cook coke, because that was all she knew. There was one meal that she made and made well.

Parmesan chicken with cream spinach and Spanish rice. It was my father's favorite dish. I think it was because it was the only one my mother cooked on his birthday. When I got downstairs, we got right to business. Marta, the housekeeper helped me maneuver around the kitchen and cut up things that needed to be cut up. I didn't know what was going on with Staten, but I wanted to be there for him. He had been there for me when I needed him, and this was my time to return the favor. Hearing that he and Liberty broke up didn't excite me like I thought it would. Mainly because I knew how much he cared for that woman. He loved everything about Liberty, so knowing that they ended shit, made me hurt for him. How could I tell him that I had a crush on him while he was grieving a break up? I couldn't do it, so I would rather keep my mouth shut and play the role of the concerned friend, which in fact was true because I was concerned about him.

I sprinkled the garnish on top of the food and then smiled at my hard work. I was so happy that I didn't burn anything and had to rely on Marta to whip something up. What cooking this meal taught me was that I needed to learn how to make other recipes because this one was going to get tired if he wanted me to cook for him again.

"What's all this?" Staten broke my concentration from getting my iron chef on.

"I figured I would cook us dinner. They sat a table on the beach for us to eat." He didn't look happy, excited, or even shocked that I could cook.

"Nah, I'm gonna go upstairs and get some sleep for tomorrow." Before I could utter another word, he was jogging up the stairs to his suite.

"You cook all this food for him... you like him," Marta had to add her two cents. She was cool and all, but I didn't need her calling me out right now.

"Shh, I need to think," I told her and paced the floor.

He didn't even see my outfit because I was behind the counter with an apron on. My hair was pulled up in my usual bun, so he didn't see how much effort I put into this. I wanted to call my sister and get her advice, but I knew she would tell me to leave the situation alone and that wasn't what I wanted to talk about right this moment. I just wanted her to give me advice since this was more up her lane.

"Bring the food to his room. Set the table on his balcony," I told Marta and went to get refreshed in my room. I heard Staten barking about something, so I went down the hall and saw him asking Marta what the fuck she and the two men were doing. "You're going to eat. I get you're feeling a way, but you're gonna eat." He turned and looked at me. If this was a cartoon, his mouth would have hit the ground. I could tell from the look on his face that he was very pleased with what stood before him.

"How you gonna just force yourself up in my room?" he smirked.

"Just like this," I walked past him and went to directing Marta and the guys on how to set everything up. Once they were done, I sat down.

"I was about to shower."

"Go shower... I'll wait out here," I replied, not taking my eyes off my cellphone.

He disappeared to shower, and I sat on the balcony and enjoyed the cool breeze and beautiful view of the sun shining. A private beach was something people dreamed of, and here Staten Davis was with one. The shit was beautiful and would been even more perfect if this was a baecation instead of a work trip. My cellphone pulled me from my thoughts. I sighed when I saw my mother's number pop across the screen.

"Hey Mami, what's up?"

"I'm well. How's everything going?"

"Good. I'm learning a lot. Thank you for trusting me with coming."

She chuckled. "Of course. When you get back when need to talk. I've heard something and want to speak to you face to face about it," she told me.

"Tell me now."

"No. I'll see you when you return home. We'll talk then."

"Alright," I agreed. My anxiety was too bad for her to call and tell me that we needed to speak, but not tell me what the subject was about.

"Remember this is business, Maliah," she reminded me like I hadn't already known previous to us arriving.

"Always," I replied and ended the call just as Staten was coming out the bathroom in a pair of sweat Nike shorts and without a shirt on. Staten wasn't ripped like he spent all day in the gym, but he damn sure looked good enough to eat, lick, and suck on.

"Business call?"

"Yeah, had to tie up some loose ends while I waited for you to hurry," I lied.

He sat down and looked at the food. "Damn, this looks good," he complimented. "I'm trying to act like I'm used to seeing you like this, but damn you look different as fuck."

I cut into my chicken and took a bite. "Good different, or bad different?"

"Good for sure. Why you never wear your hair like that on the regular?"

"Cause what I look like walking around like this when I got business to handle? Niggas already be trying to fuck me, imagine if I walked around like this," I snickered and finished chewing my food.

"Yeah, you right about that.... Still, when you're not working you don't never dress like this," he pointed out.

I didn't get dressed up because I was always working.

Whenever I did have time for myself, I was always in the house catching up on missed sleep. Even when Mariah would make me go out, I would toss on anything just to go so she didn't complain about missed sister time. Getting dressed up like this was a privilege and I honestly did it because I wanted to see if he would notice. If he didn't notice, that meant he never paid me attention. In the kitchen, I had my hair pulled back and I was behind the counter, so he didn't notice that I was dressed up. Make-up had never been my strong suit, so I didn't even bother trying to paint my face and end up looking like a damn clown.

"Never had a reason to..." I allowed my voice to trail off and looked out onto the view. It was true, I never had a reason or a person to get dressed up for.

I never wanted to be the one who claimed to be jealous of my sister and I wasn't. She had everything she wanted with Trac. He adored, love and spoiled her, even though he knew she could do for herself. As much as I gave her shit for wanting out the game and just being a wife, I kind of admired her too. She was so strong on wanting to be better than this life and fighting for love. It got old coming home to an empty place. It was the reason I stalled on getting my own place for a while. At least when I lived with my parents I could come home to the house-keepers, butlers, and staff. When I entered through my front door of my own crib, I was greeted by silence and more silence.

"You got a reason right here." He looked into my eyes.

"Seriously?"

"Hell yeah. I'm tired of looking at that damn hair pulled into a big bun," he laughed, which caused me to smile. "Nah, I'm fucking with you. You don't need a nigga to dress up and be you. Fuck these niggas."

"Thank you." I took a sip of champagne and leaned back in my chair. "What's going on with you? You're not yourself."

"How do you know I'm not myself?"

"Because I'm around you all the time. I know when you're not yourself and since we've arrived you haven't said more than one word to me. Actually, tonight is the first time you've said something since we've landed."

He started eating his food and then took a sip of his champagne. "I just been going through a lot of shit." He was short.

"Since when you can't kick it and let me know what's going on? I already know about you and Lib, that's not what's bothering you, right?"

"Hell yeah. She ended shit because I questioned her on some fuck shit she was doing. Relationships are fucking overrated."

"Not when they're done right," I added. "Liberty is probably scared and ended things because she doesn't want to hurt you."

"How the fuck didn't she want to hurt me? She broke the fuck up with me," he pushed his plate away.

Seeing a man take a break up hard was kind of refreshing. Us women automatically assumed that they didn't care in a break up. I know for a fact that I thought they went on about their day like nothing happened. Seeing how broken up Staten was about this break-up showed me that he cared for Liberty. He wasn't the type to get hung up on shit, and seeing that he was legit heartbroken about this, I knew that she was special to him.

"I'm sorry," was all I could muster. I was no good at comforting my own twin, so how was I going to comfort him?

"Yeah, me too. I'm sorry that I love so fucking hard and can't get that shit back." He sniffled and looked away. "I put so much into that relationship. Damn, it hurts when I think of how I revealed so much of myself to her. When the fuck is it going to be time for me to be loved. I look at Priest and Ghost and see how much Free and Justice love them. They would lay down and die for my brothers and I can't even get a fucking call back after she gets off from work. What the fuck am I doing wrong? Why am I not enough?"

I was hurt seeing him breaking down like this. The tears that fell down his cheeks were real. Removing myself from my chair, I leaned down between his legs and forced him to look me in the face. "You listen to me... you're enough, Shaliq. I don't care what she's going through, but I care about you. You're enough. Liberty is a fool not to see what a good man that you are. You care about everyone before yourself. How many times have you dropped everything and was there for me? You've been there for me when I've needed you the most. If Liberty can't see that, then maybe she's not the type of woman you should be with. God has a way of removing people from our lives. We question it, but then he makes his reason more clear as time passes." I held onto his hands and stared him in the eyes.

Tears were coming to my eyes just talking about how much of a good man he was. Staten had his fair share of problems. He wasn't the most perfect man walking the streets, but he was most definitely one of the realest. When he loved you, he would go to the end of the world to make sure you're good. I watch this man pay out the ass for an expensive rehab to put Liberty in, all because he loved her. Even then, he was prepared to spend more time apart from her if she needed to stay in rehab longer.

He looked down at me and wiped the tear the fell from my eyes. "Why you crying?"

"Because I love your ass, Staten," I stood up and walked over to the banister. "I've always loved you, but always sat back and watched these chicks play you."

It was silent. Did I cross the line? Should I have shut my mouth and continued to comfort him? I was the most confident person when holding a gun and handling my shit in the streets. When it came to men, feelings and all that other shit, I had this insecure side that caused me to question everything. It was one of the main reasons I avoided dating. I couldn't imagine opening myself up and getting played like some basic bitch. Shit like that would cause me to pull out my gun and bust a few shots in a nigga.

I felt his hand around my waist, and he stood to the left of me. His hand was still around my waist. "You don't think I know when someone is feeling me?" he had a smirk fixed up on his lips.

"You knew this whole time?"

"Shit is mad obvious," he turned me to look up in his eyes. Each time I tried to look off, he used his index finger to bring my face back toward his. "Don't be shy now."

"I'm not," I lied. My panties were wet, and I was sure I had beads of sweat coming down my face. This was what he did to me. He caused me to turn into this little girl that I tried hard not to be. My words got all twisted, I thought about what I was going to say twice before I spoke, and I was constantly trying not to seem like a little girl compared to the women he dated. Even if I acted way mature than them.

"Be real with me, Maliah. You always keep it a hundred. It's low-key cute as shit seeing you like this," he laughed.

"Weren't you just crying a second ago?"

He shrugged. "What can I say? I'm an emotional ass nigga, now you know."

I tried to walk off, but he grabbed my hand and pulled me close to him. Holding my face, he bent down and kissed me on the lips. Electricity shot through my body and charged up my energy or something. Our lips separated and I looked at him. Standing on my toes, I put my lips back on his and wrapped my arms around his neck. We kissed and grabbed at each other's tongue like it was the last supper. I sucked on his tongue, he sucked on mine as he grabbed my ass. I felt him hike me up and lift me up. Wrapping my legs around his body, I kissed his neck while he sucked on mine. We finally came up for air and I stared at him as he held me up like it wasn't nothing.

"Once we step into that room... you can't undo anything. You sure you want this?" he asked as he kissed me on the lips, chin, and neck.

Moaning, I tossed my head back and allowed him to feast on my neck. "Yes, I want it," I moaned out.

He walked into the bedroom and closed the glass doors, leaving us in a completely dark room. Staten laid me down onto the bed gently and I stared up at him with one leg extended out and one leg curled up. He lowered himself over me and kissed me on the lips as he pulled down my jumper. With no bra, my breast came out once the jumper was pulled down to my stomach. My body wasn't something I bragged about. Mariah always complained how I had the perfect body. I never understood since we were identical twins. She claimed that my abs, butt, and thighs were perfect without any cellulite. I didn't know what eyes she was looking through because I had cellulite all through up and down my damn butt and thighs. Staten took a nipple into his mouth and swirled his tongue all around it. The motion sent shutters through my entire soul. I would lay in bed and dream about what it would be like to have Staten. Just one night, I wasn't picky. It felt unreal that we were in his room about to have sex.

With my nipple still in his mouth, he pulled the rest of my jumpsuit off, and opened my legs. He patted my pussy and the material of my mesh thong and his hands caused me to squirm around.

"You wet as fuck." He pulled my thong to the side and stuck his fingers inside me slowly. I wanted this for so long and I was trying to get away. What was wrong with me? This was what I wanted. Staten was what I wanted, no he was who I needed and craved.

"Sorry." Sorry? What the hell was wrong with me? Who the

hell apologizes because they're wet? Me! That's who. I closed my eyes and enjoyed the pleasure he was putting through my body. If his fingers felt like this, what did his actual dick feel like? Staten could blow on me and I probably would have cum.

"You good... real good," he moaned out and kissed me on the neck while his fingers still explored my insides. He hit a spot and my legs flew open like a car door, I gyrated my hips to chase this feeling he was bringing onto my body.

I didn't want to be a rebound. Was I a rebound? I didn't want to be the girl who helped him clear his mind of Liberty for a brief second. I wanted to be the woman who he has always secretly wanted but was too afraid to step to. Why were these thoughts going through my mind?

"Oh my God!" I screamed out when I felt his lips down on my second pair of lips. He looked up at me with this lustful look as he bent down and slurped from my personal river. With all he had been doing, I knew I was probably accumulating a small river down there. Staten didn't seem to mind as he slapped his tongue like a cat getting a taste of milk.

My hands searched for something...anything to grab. It felt like my body was going to float over this bed in a few if I didn't find something to keep me grounded. He pushed my legs further and further apart as his head dug deeper and deeper into me. If someone would have walked in, you would have thought I was giving birth to Staten's ass.

"Shittttt," he said while still giving me the business. The vibrations sent chills through my damn spine. "Stop trying to run, you wanted this and I'm gonna give it to you," he groaned as he stood up and dropped his basketball shorts and boxers. His dick sprung out like a damn coil spring in a mattress. "Ain't no coming back from this," he warned me. Still, I laid there ready for him to break down my walls and re-build them again.

He climbed on top of me and pushed my legs apart. I felt his dick tapping at my door. He was gentle as he entered inch by inch inside of me. Staten was blessed below, and he knew it. The shit just added to his cocky ass. With his bowleg stance and sweat pants, you could see just how big his print was without ever having to feel the shit. Mariah was the one who put me onto dick prints. Staten's was my favorite to look at. It was like he had no clue that I could see the entire silhouette of his dick.

I grabbed hold of his shoulders because it started to hurt. Tears fell from my eyes as he entered and broke my hymen. I continued to claw at his back as he stroked me nice and slow. Whoever lied and said that it felt better after the cherry was broke lied like hell. It wasn't something I was enjoying because of the pain. I also knew if I wasn't in pain, I probably would have been moaning and tossing this pussy all over the room. He kissed me on the neck as he continued because he could see the pain etched all over my face. Holding onto him, I allowed him to fuck me into womanhood. My virginity was officially gone, and I didn't know whether to cry, call my sister, or just ride this wave out until he was done. Mariah always teased that I would be a virgin until I was in my thirties. And, I had to admit that I thought the same thing too.

"You tight as shit," he groaned out as he lifted my left leg and pinned it to the head board. I watched as the muscles in his arms flexed with each stroke he delivered. He started off slow, but his pace had quickened. He bit down on his bottom lip as his concentration took over. I laid there and enjoyed the ride he was taking me on. Sex wasn't something I was about to pretend I knew about. It was a subject that I got to live through when Mariah spoke about she and Trac. It wasn't something I had ever tried, so I was fine with laying here and allowing him to teach me some things.

He collapsed beside me and laid on the pillow. My virginity was gone, and I felt even more like a woman. My virginity was something precious to me and I didn't want to just give it to anyone. Men worked so hard to try and take a woman's virginity and never put half the effort into trying to get to know them. It didn't matter that me and Staten probably would never fuck again. This was enough and I was satisfied with it being him that took my virginity.

"How you feel?" he asked as he laid beside me. "You was just screaming my damn name, lay closer," he laughed.

I tucked the cover around my body and moved closer to him. "I feel good. How do you feel?"

"Like a nigga that busted a good ass nut," he smiled. "On the real, you know your moms could never find out about this."

"Do you really think I sit and talk about sex with my mother? You've met my mother; do you really think she wants to sit around and hear about sex?"

"Yeah, you right. Nobody can find out about this," he made sure to add.

"Why? You ashamed of me or something?"

"Nah... I just don't want to ruin what we have. When other people get involved that's when shit ends up being misunderstood or turned into a mess. It's nice having something for myself," he rolled on top of me and stared down at me.

"To yourself, huh?" I repeated to myself.

"Yeah. I'm a low-key nigga, and I feel like lately my business been out there. Between Liberty and Chanel, everybody know my business before I do."

"True." He kissed me on the lips.

"Liah, on the real, it wasn't until you became legal and started working with me, that I saw that you weren't that little girl anymore. I know that you can go toe to toe with a grown man but get silly when someone compliments you. Small shit, I know." He sealed his words with another kiss. "I'm not gonna sit here and tell you that I want to jump into a relationship with you, cause I don't want to hurt you."

"Then what are you telling me?"

I sighed, preparing myself to hear the bullshit he was about to tell me. "I'm still in love with Liberty. It would be selfish of me to start something with you, knowing I'm still in love with Liberty and about to welcome a new baby with Chanel. I couldn't drag you into my mess. I got too much love for you."

I had to respect his honesty. Other niggas would have lied and tried to act like no other woman existed except for me. Staten was honest and told me what I already knew. He wasn't over Liberty and I didn't want to be the woman that he used as a distraction from her. Yet, I was so in with Staten that I would happily be his distraction if he needed me to be.

"I don't want to be used. Keep it real with me. I'm not looking for a relationship either, but I don't want to be lied to like we're in one. Keep it a hundred with me and I promise we'll be good."

"Bet." He pulled the sheets off me. "I'm bout to teach your ass how to ride dick, you ready?" nodding my head, I prepared for the rollercoaster ride he was about to take me on physically and mentally. I would be a fool to think this would be easy or I would be able to keep my emotions in check.

10

Liberty
Don't grab me in public, but ride me in private – Wale

I was shocked that I hadn't heard from Staten in a little while. He went from still calling and texting almost every day to dropping off the face of the earth. I wasn't about to press him or hit him up either. Breaking up with Staten was hard and I thought about him every day. I'm just tired of the constant daddy behavior. He acted like he was my father and I was tired of feeling like I had to hide every and anything from him. The thing that made it worse was that he didn't understand where I was coming from. All he could do is accuse me of shit that I hadn't done or try and search my car and house. That wasn't a relationship and I had to get out of it and end things with him. My sisters didn't even know, and I knew today at lunch I had to sit down and talk to them about it. It was only a matter of time before they found out. The first week I cried my eyes out and stayed cooped up in the house. Despite it being my decision, it was hard ending things with him. Staten was the love of my life. Even before he became overly protective, we had a good time together. He was my love and best friend all wrapped up into one. Even now, I missed having him around to talk.

Our relationship had gone from something that I enjoyed having to something that I felt I had to work ten times harder to keep. Relationships are hard and take work, yet this one felt like it was taking me under, and I couldn't catch a break. The other reason was that I didn't want to let him down. With me relapsing, I knew it would break his heart. How could I face him knowing I was back using? I never gave a fuck about what anyone said, but that man... I cared about his disappointment in me. It was something that I didn't want to witness. It was easier to end things and go about our lives like nothing happened. I killed my engine and walked into the restaurant. Both Justice and Freedom wouldn't allow me to get out of this. They claimed I had been distant and wanted to see me. What was so wrong with having my own space and life away from them?

When I was escorted to the table, they were both already digging into the bread the waiter had provided. Those hoes never waited for me before they were pregnant, and they definitely weren't going to wait while being pregnant. When they saw me, they stopped stuffing their faces long enough to get up and hug me really quick. I sat across from the both of them and grabbed a piece of bread. I couldn't remember the last time I had put some food into my body.

"I feel like I haven't seen you in years," Freedom started in. I knew it was going to be her who brought up the amount of time we hadn't seen each other.

"Been working and trying to spend as much time with Chance as I can." It wasn't a lie. I was really working and going to visit Chance whenever I had the time. Ty had become someone new in my life that I liked spending time with too.

"Too busy to catch up with your pregnant sisters?" she countered.

"Why are you trying to make this something that it's not? I've been busy and have a life, just like the both of you have lives," I snapped.

"It's nice being out with you. We have to stop letting so much time pass before we get together," Justice jumped in before this turned all the way left. With the look Free had on her face, I could tell she was about to make it an argument.

"Yeah, we need to stop doing that," I grabbed the menu and looked it over. "I think I'm gonna get the chef's salad." I placed it back down and stared at the both of them.

"A salad?" Free asked.

"Yeah, I don't want nothing too heavy. I'm trying to watch my figure."

"You're looking thin, Lib," Justice made sure to add. "I'm not saying you're not eating, but you should get more than a salad."

"This is why I don't come to have lunch with the both of you. Instead of having lunch with my sisters, I feel like I'm having lunch with mommy. Even she's not as bad as the two of you."

"I'm sorry. We just want to make sure that you're good. Is that a crime?" Free bit a piece of her bread.

"Yes, when the person keeps telling you that they're fine. I'm alright and when I'm not, I'll let you all know."

"Deal," Justice said. "I think Priest may be cheating on me."

Me and Free both laughed, while she looked on confused. "Cheating on you? That man loves the hell out of you. Priest would cut off his foot before he cheats on you."

"I agree," I added.

"He has this ex that he didn't tell me about. She popped back into his life and now he's been acting really funny. We got into an argument last week, and he still hasn't sat down so we can talk about it."

"Has he been busy?" Free asked.

"Yes, but he always makes time to talk out our arguments. I don't care that you both are laughing; I know what I feel and it's real." She leaned back in her chair and rubbed her stomach.

The waiter came and took our orders and then left to fulfill them. "You really need to stop stressing yourself about stuff that doesn't matter. Do you think Priest is stupid enough to mess up everything the both of you have built? He loves the shit out of you and you're going to ruin a good thing by over-thinking shit. He's not your past," I told her.

"Why doesn't he want to talk? What was the fight about?" Free wanted to know.

"Kiss. She leaves the baby with me and he complained about me constantly allowing her to do that."

"Well, is he really wrong? Kiss had that baby, not you. Why should you be raising him while she all over Staten Island with Reese?"

I sipped my lemonade. "Yeah, and the crazy thing is that Reese be wanting her to be with her son. You have to stop making things so easy for her. What's going to happen when you have your daughter? Is she gonna help you like you've been helping her? Priest is not wrong."

Justice rolled her eyes and I could tell this was causing the tension in her household. She wanted to help everyone, and no one ever wanted to give her any help in return. Kiss was using her so she would be able to hang with her friends when she wanted to. That girl had that baby and realized that the shit was harder than she thought. Especially since her baby father was murdered.

"All I'm trying to do is help her and he's getting an attitude about it. I slipped and mentioned how she wouldn't need as much help if he didn't kill her baby father."

Both me and Free gasped. "I would have slapped your ass.

Why would you say that?" Free dabbed her bread into the balsamic oil mix and shook her head in disbelief.

"It slipped out of my mouth," she sighed. "Do you really think I wanted to say that to him?"

"Well, it came out your mouth," I countered. "No wonder he doesn't want to talk about it. He did something hard as fuck. He was protecting his family and tearing a family apart at the same time. You think he doesn't live with that shit on his mind every day, or when he lays eyes on his nephew? Justice, you can be selfish sometimes. If your man doesn't want you helping out so much with *his* niece, then you need to fall back and let them work that shit out."

"Exactly. How you gonna tell him what he needs to do with his own family? You need to be worried about that damn baby, and not Kiss's baby. Period."

"Period, Pooh!" Me and Free both fell out laughing while Justice had this grill on her face. We didn't give a damn that she was angry. Right was right and wrong was wrong. She shouldn't have been arguing about what Priest should do with his niece that he raised. It wasn't her place and she was dead ass wrong.

"Anyway, what's new with you?" Free focused in on me. "I miss talking and catching up with you."

"Me and Staten broke up," I revealed. It was time for them to know before someone else told them.

Both of their dramatic asses gasped and put their hands to their mouth. "What? Why? How?" Justice stammered.

"We both were too busy, and I was tired of feeling like I was his project or something."

"Project or something? What does that even mean?" Leave it to Free to want to know more. She couldn't just take that we broke up, she had to know why and dissect every little thing I said.

"He was acting too much like my sober coach instead of my nigga. I'm tired of having to tell him everything that I was doing, or him showing up randomly at my house to check it. It was too much, and I was tired of dealing with it. Things changed once I went to rehab and I was trying to hold onto something that was dead."

"What changed? You both were good and now you're telling me that things were dead?"

"Free, shit can change. I'm allowed to change how I feel about someone... It didn't work out, case closed."

"Do you think it's a chance that you both can work it out?" Justice wondered.

"Only God knows... right now, I'm not trying to be with anyone. I need to focus on myself and don't need to have someone clocking my every move."

"He cares about you. I'm bout to cal—"

"No, the fuck you're not. If I said I broke up with someone, then that's what it is. How are you gonna go and try to call him? You're my sister, not his. I don't care that you're fucking his big brother and about to have a baby with him either," I pointed my finger in Free's face. "I told you that we're broken up, give us both space without asking a million damn questions. This is our business, not yours."

"Get your damn finger out my fucking face. Second, you broke up with him because he fucking cared about you. That's stupid as fuck."

"No what's stupid is that the both of you think that you can control my damn life. I don't ever give my opinion on your relationships unless it's asked for. Why can't I ever get the same respect back? You both don't know what went on in our relationship or why I really wanted to end things, so how are you both judging me? I didn't want to continue with the relationship and that's my choice. Will we ever get back together? Who knows?"

The waiter put our food down and I grabbed my fork and dug into my salad. "I'm sad that you both aren't together anymore. Staten hasn't even mentioned anything about it either."

"Well, there you have it. He hasn't spoken about it, so let's just leave it alone."

"It's something more and you're just not telling us. How does one just want to end a relationship without trying to work on things first?"

"Because I'm fucking allowed to, Free!" I slammed my hands on the table and screamed. The entire restaurant turned and looked at our table.

The outburst wasn't something I had planned on doing, but Free was pissing me off with her suspicions. Why couldn't it be that I didn't want to be in the relationship anymore? Why did it have to be some hidden motive when it came to her? Yes, I broke up with him because I was back using, and I couldn't stand to see his face if he ever found out. It wasn't only that either, I was tired of being treated like a damn child in my relationship. Even when it came to my sisters, they acted like I was this fucking child and I wasn't. Why couldn't I just end a relationship and they be there for me? It was the main reason I kept shit to myself and didn't deal with them.

"I'm tired of fucking explaining myself to the both of you bitches. I'm done, leave me alone and send me a birth announcement when the both of you drop.... I'm out," I dropped my fork onto the table, grabbed my purse and headed out of the restaurant, leaving the both of them stunned.

All I came to do was have a nice lunch with my sisters and they always turned it into something more than that. Why couldn't they ever update me on their lives? Free had a baby with a heart condition, yet she was so busy in my damn business when she should have been worried about her own life. Justice has a high-risk pregnancy, and she minding my business too. She should have been concerned about if Priest was fucking another woman after the foul shit she had said. I jumped into my truck and pulled off. These bitches weren't about to ruin my damn day.

"FUCK, YES!" I screamed out as my hands were planted on his chest and I rode his dick like I was trying to win the Kentucky Derby. His hands were wrapped around my waist and every so often he would slap my ass just to see the ripple effect. "I'm about to..." my words trailed off as I came and rolled off of him onto the bed.

"Damn, you be fucking the shit out of me," Ty laughed as he laid there. We were both sweaty and had been at it for over three hours— nonstop.

His stamina and mine matched up perfectly. We could have gone for another hour, but my legs were weak from busting so many nuts. Fucking hit different when you did a line of coke and had two shots of bourbon. Ty didn't know I did coke, but we both did shots of bourbon and was ready to go after kissing. I covered my body with the sheet filled with wet spots and turned on my side to look at him. Ty would have been a perfect man to be with. He was smart, rich, and was about his business. Any woman would have been proud to have him as her man. Things were complicated because he wanted me as his woman, and I wasn't there with him. I couldn't jump into another relationship with another man. Shit, I needed time to deal with my own shit. Plus, I wasn't ready to open myself up to another man the way I had to Staten. Since the day I was in his strip-club, and he had showed me his other club in the city, we had been cool. We started fucking and that's when things picked up. I learned how although he owned clubs, he had other businesses too and was a pillar of his community. He donated to charities and attended these fancy events.

Staten was a good man too, but he had his demons and wasn't perfect either. With Ty, this man was too damn perfect to be with. He was looking for a wife, not a woman who had a drug habit. He often brought up taking our relationship a step closer since he broke his celibacy. My plan wasn't to turn him out on this good pussy, it just happened. I laughed because he went from waiting for the right one, to fucking with me. I could tell for sure I wasn't the woman for him. We weren't a match. I couldn't be perfect, and I couldn't be this trophy wife who stood on his arm and smiled all night. I had never been the type and I couldn't pretend to be the type, even if that meant for a nigga that was possibly worth it and deserved it.

"I have this event to go to tonight... I want you to come as my date," he brought up. It seemed like this was the only time he brought up having an event and wanting to invite me to them.

I sighed and rolled my eyes. He laughed when he saw my expression. "What's so funny?"

He rubbed my face with his thumb and smiled. "You. Every time I want to invite you somewhere you act all weird like I'm asking you to get married."

"I don't think I'm ready to be on your arm as your date."

"Nah, going out into public with me makes it real. Going to the club doesn't really matter but going to an event would make this real."

"No, why you trying to act like you know me," I laughed and tossed the pillow at him. "I told you that I just got out of a relationship."

"What that got to do with me?" he stared at me seriously.

I rubbed his chest and pulled the sheets off me so I could go in for another round, just to shut him up about this. He gently removed my hands and stared at me. "Why are you being all serious now?"

"Because I want to know that my time isn't being wasted."

"How do you figure your time is being wasted?"

He leaned up and sat on the edge of the bed with his back

facing me. "Liberty, I know you just got out of a situation and I'm not rushing for us to be something. Still, I'm not just trying to be fucking you with no clear direction on where we're going... feel me?"

"I hear you. Right now, we're having sex and getting to know each other. Once I'm ready for the next step, you'll be the first to know," I lied. There would be no other step. I wasn't trying to be roped into a relationship with Ty. This nigga wanted a wife and I wasn't the wifey type.

"Ight," he replied, being dry.

I crawled over to him and wrapped my arms around his neck and kissed his neck. "I'm here and I'm trying... I told you that it's hard for me to open up to people. Patience is everything to me and when I feel pressured, I back myself into a wall and build a bigger barrier," I said in-between kisses.

"I hear you." He took my hand and placed a kiss upon the top of it. "I gotta few meetings today before this event.... Will I see you tomorrow?"

I kissed him once more. "Yep. Call me and I'll come," I told him. "You sure you need to go right now?" I laid back on the bed and opened my legs. Patting my pussy, I grinned at him. From his dick, I could tell he wanted to dive in for another swim.

"Ight once more," he growled as he leaped onto the bed, and I giggled feeling him slide right up inside of me again.

After going another round, Ty's assistant came knocking on his door trying to get him to his meetings on time. Ty told me to stay at his house for however long I wanted to stay. He lived in a huge mansion in Princeton, New Jersey. The house was beautiful and told me how much money this nigga was really getting. What bugged me out was that he lived here alone. He had no children or anything. I never understood why people bought these huge homes and lived alone. I had some clothes packed so I tossed on some clothes after my shower and headed out to my car. Today was my day to spend with Chance and I was already running behind.

Just left the crib and I'm already missing you. I smiled at Ty's text message. He always sent me sweet messages like that. I hated that we could never be more than what we were now. It was selfish of me to keep him to myself knowing I could never be what he was looking for in a woman. I could get used to having chefs cook for me, shopping all day and doing nothing all day. It wasn't like Staten never offered any of this. He told me numerous times to quit my job and I always fought him on it.

Missing you too. Have a good day. See you soon I replied before tossing my phone onto the passenger seat and pulling out of his iron gates. I turned the radio up and cruised to go pick up my baby boy. We were going to shop and hang out for the entire weekend. He had been calling me and because of work I wasn't able to come last weekend, but this weekend I put personal time in so I could spend time with him. I hadn't heard from my sisters and I wasn't expecting to. As much as I loved them, I realized that I needed a break from them and that was alright. It was fine to choose me and not deal with someone else's negative opinions. If they knew that I was sleeping with Ty, they would have so much to say. It pained me that I couldn't come and talk to my sisters about things going on in my life without them judging or trying to convince me what I was doing was wrong. To avoid all of that, I just stayed away from them. I hit the green button on my screen and answered the unfamiliar number I had seen.

"Hey, who is this?" I answered as I tapped my hand on the steering wheel and nodded my head to the music that was playing in the background.

"It's me. Staten."

"What number is this? I don't have it saved."

"My new number. I wanted to come by to grab my gym bag I left there," he replied.

"New number? Why'd you get a new number?" It wasn't my place to ask, but I did because I was curious to know why he had gotten a new number.

"Let me save this numb—"

"Nah, this number will be changed soon too... You home? I can swing by and you can bring it downstairs."

"Oh. No, I'm heading to hang with Chance for the weekend... if you want, you can come chill too. He's been asking about you."

"Nah, I'm straight. Hit me up when you're back in the city. Tell Chance I said what's good?" he said and ended the call. The way he ended the call so abruptly had me in my feelings. Why was he acting so funny now? And why wasn't he begging and pleading to be with me? I knew he didn't want this break up, so why act like you're happy about it now? I sighed and fixed my sunglasses

Me and Chance were in Target grabbing some things for dinner. It was going to be just me and him since my aunt went away with her little boyfriend for the weekend. She needed the time away because she spent all her time doing everything for Chance. I sniffled and wiped my nose and grabbed some white rice.

"Mommy, are you sick like before? Do you have to go back to that place again?" Chance randomly asked as he played with his toy he just had to get.

I quickly turned around. "No, baby. Why would you say that?"

"You keep sniffling. I know last time you were sick you sniffled too." I didn't give this boy enough credit. He was way too smart for his own good. His teachers always said he was very observant, and it wasn't until now that I realized just how much he actually was.

"No, I'm just cold in here that's all. Stop worrying, kid," I smirked, and he giggled and continued messing with his Iron man toy.

I blew out a small breath and continued to pick up things for dinner tonight. If Chance noticed, I needed to get my shit together because it was no telling who else could tell and just wasn't saying anything to me.

Staten

IF YOU TAKE your love away from me, I'll go crazy, I'll go insane –
Black Street

"WHERE YOU GOING DRESSED LIKE THAT?" I asked as pulled Maliah back into my arms. She giggled and then looked me in the eyes. When she looked at me, I could feel how much she cared for me. It felt good as fuck to feel what I was putting out all this time.

"Quit playing. I have on sweats and a crop top," she batted those long ass eyelashes of hers. "I'm going shopping with my sister. I haven't seen her since we got back from Belize," she explained as I kissed her on the neck.

"Bet. Hit me when you heading back to the crib."

"Lock up my shit, Staten," she threatened as she grabbed her wallet to head out the door. I watched as her ass switched in those tight ass sweats while licking my lips.

If you told me that me and Maliah would have been fucking around, I would have called you crazy. I noticed some shit she used to do, but never paid it any attention. On the real, I didn't think we would mesh. She was too much like her mother and I couldn't be with a woman who was so emotionally unavailable. Seeing her like this was different. A good different. Since Belize, we had been fucking like no other. I been wearing her virgin ass out and teaching her just how I liked to be fucked. I stood against the kitchen counter for a minute before I went to her room to change into some clothes. When I called Liberty earlier, I was surprised by how unbothered I was. I needed my gym bag because I had my other burner in that bag. If I didn't need that gun, I wouldn't have made an effort to come over there to get it. I looked down at my phone and saw Chanel was calling me. She was another one I had been avoiding. After I finished handling business, I always found my way to Maliah's door. She brought peace to me. She conducted herself one way out in the streets, but once she crossed the threshold of her crib, she was different.

She wore booty shorts, cleaned while singing to Spanish music and cooked. I'm not gonna front, she didn't cook all that well and only knew one, maybe two solid recipes. It didn't matter because she was trying. When I got a call from Chanel, she didn't trip of get an attitude. Shit was cool with us and had me thinking that I wouldn't have minded being in a relationship with her. I pressed the green button and placed my phone to my ear. If she wasn't so far along, I wouldn't have answered each time she fucking called.

"What's good, Chanel?"

"I'm heading to the hospital, my water broke," she replied, calm as shit. I thought women went crazy when their water broke. She was on the phone talking like she wasn't about to push a damn baby out of her stomach.

"What? You good? The head not out, right?" I ran into Maliah's room and grabbed my clothes from yesterday. I hopped around on one foot trying to put my basketball shorts on.

"Yes, I'm fine. You forget I'm a labor and delivery nurse," she did a nervous laugh. "My mom is driving me to the hospital."

"Bet. I'm leaving out right now and heading there."

Chanel was super prepared when it came to this pregnancy. She made us take a tour of the same hospital she fucking worked at and even opted into getting a birthing suite because she wanted peace while birthing. I know she did that shit because she knew I would cover the bill. If she didn't have me, she would have been having that baby down in those same small ass rooms she had coached many pregnant women in.

"Where are you coming from?"

"Why is that important?" I questioned. Why the fuck was my location important when she was about to have my seed? "Look, I'm heading to the hospital right now. Sit tight," I told her and ended the call.

My damn hands and shit were shaking. I was about to become a fucking father. I knew this baby was coming, but now it was ten times more real that my baby girl was coming into the world. I was about to be somebody's daddy. The thought alone had my heart beating out my chest and shit. I set the alarm to Maliah's crib and then jumped into my whip. While I peeled out, I dialed Ghost's number, I drove like a bat out of hell out the complex.

"What's good?" he answered, he sounded like he was half asleep.

Since I found out about him having cancer, me and Priest had been switching days on bringing him to his treatments. Ghost was big on not trying to appear weak in front of us. I hated that he felt like he had to be strong all the time. We were his brothers and we wanted to be there for him and hold him down like he had always done for us.

"You sleep? I can call back if you want," I stopped at the stop sign.

"Nah, I was just taking a nap. I had chemo and that shit be having me tired... what's good?" it sounded like he was sitting up in the bed or the couch, wherever he was at.

"You good?"

"Nigga, yeah. What the hell happened?"

"Chanel about to go have the baby. Her water broke and

she's headed to the hospital now," I blurted. It was hard as fuck trying to hold this shit in while asking how he was doing.

"Word? Congrats, you're about to be a pops, nigga!" he laughed and clapped into the phone. "How you feeling?"

"Scared as shit. I'm scared as shit to be a father, man. What if I fail her?"

He chuckled slightly. "Shaliq, you could never fail someone. I watch you with your nieces and nephew and you're always on their asses to be better. Have you ever failed me?"

"I don't think I have."

"Nah, you never have."

"I did. Summer," I revealed. Still to this day, I felt like I let my brother down. His prized procession, I had failed to protect. "With the life I live, how can I protect my own daughter if I couldn't protect my niece?" I added.

Ghost sighed. "You risked your life for your nieces. Nigga, you forgot you was riddled with bullets? Because you threw yourself over the top of them, you were able to save Rain, and for that I can't thank you enough. As bad as it hurts, it was time for her to go home with God. It hurts to this day, but I'm a peace knowing that my baby is resting."

It was a sigh of relief hearing that my brother didn't hold any resentment toward me. I was the one responsible for his daughter and I failed him. I failed my niece too. The shit was on my head almost every day.

"I just didn't wan—"

"Stop thinking like this," he cut me off. "Go and have that baby girl. I'm sure Summer is whispering in her ear to give you hell soon as she enters the world," he joked.

"Damn, it's like that?"

"Hell yeah. You'll see soon enough that this daddy shit isn't for the weak. It's the weak that run away and leave the woman to raise these kids. I'm proud of you, baby boy... go and be there for Chanel's annoying ass."

"Leave my baby mama alone."

"You'll see," he chuckled before we ended the call.

Chanel having the baby. Might be over tonight. I sent Maliah a quick message before heading to the hospital. I prayed like hell no cop pulled me over today.

Wow! Congrats and don't let her ruin this moment for you. I'm here if you need to talk, I checked Maliah's message as I headed up to Chanel's room.

When I entered the room, Chanel was already being hooked up to the IV and was in a hospital gown. She had a full face of make-up and her little friends was all around her chatting their big ass teeth. They all stopped when they saw me enter the room. Chanel's mother was in the corner on her phone.

"How was the traffic getting over here?" Chanel asked, as she swatted her friend curling her hair away.

"Good. Why you got so many people in here?" I looked at all the same bitches that were always in her ear. Half of these bitches' baby daddies were locked up or begging for me to put them on. Even before Chanel got pregnant, I told her to watch out for these bitches and she never listened.

"The baby isn't coming right away," she shot back as she ran her hands through her hair. Chanel was in here all dolled up like she was about to meet Obama or something.

"How are you, Shaliq?" Her mother finally put the phone down and acknowledged me.

"I'm good. How are you, Ms. Diana?" I questioned.

Chanel's parents didn't like me. Especially, her mother. She tolerated me as her friend, but now that I was her baby father, she wasn't pleased with Chanel or her life choices. When it came to her granddaughter, I knew she would love her like she loved Chanel. Still, that didn't mean she liked me anymore. If it was up to her, Chanel would raise that baby without me.

"How are you doing, Mr. Davis?" Chanel's doctor entered the room. "Are you ready to meet your baby girl?"

"Hell yeah. How long until she comes?"

"Since her water broke, we're waiting for her to become more dilatated. It can be awhile so get comfortable. As far as the birth, you want both your mother and Mr. Davis, correct?"

"Yep," Chanel had replied.

"Ladies... please finish up and then you'll have to wait in the family waiting room," the doctor told them.

I leaned back in the chair next to Chanel's bed. Once her hood booger friends left, we watched a few episodes of Family Feud before her contractions started coming. I held onto her and allowed her to lay her head on my shoulder. Chanel refused to get pain medicine and wanted to use some blue ball to bounce on. Her mother tried to get in and help, but I kept jumping in to help. If it was up to me, her ass would have been outside waiting for the baby to come. It was then that I remembered that I didn't call my mother. She had asked me to be a part of my daughter's birth and that shit slipped my mind. While Chanel leaned her head on my shoulder and moaned out, I sent a text to my mother.

Ma, Chanel having the baby. Come to the hospital,

Already on my way. Figured you were too nervous and forgot to call me. Gyson called me and told me, she sent a text back.

"Who gave you those hickies on your neck?" Chanel moaned out while being in pain. Why the fuck did that matter? And I told Maliah about sucking on my neck. She liked nibbling and biting on my neck.

"Stop worrying about shit that isn't important right now," I whispered to her. The last thing I wanted was to get into an argument with her mother sitting right there.

"No, tell me," she moaned out while gripping onto my shoulders. "You and Liberty back on good terms?" I forgot I hadn't told Chanel that me and Liberty had broken up.

"It's not important right now, Chanel. You and our baby is what matters right now," I tried to avoid the argument. I didn't want my baby coming into this world with an argument brewing between her parents.

"I'm so sick of you putting off.... Ouchhhhh!" she screamed and damn near took my shoulders off with the mighty strength.

"Chanel right now isn't the time for that. Let him keep his bad energy to himself," Diana had the nerve to say.

"Who the fuck bringing bad energy?" I barked. "I came in here with the sole purpose to see my daughter brought into the world."

"You never wanted this baby and it showed the entire pregnancy," she accused. I admit, I wasn't the most excited about Chanel getting pregnant. I knew she wanted a baby and I made that promise to her years ago, so I went along with it. Soon as I found out that she was pregnant, I had been there for every step of the way. Even when her petty ass liked to go ghost and ignore my calls. Her mother had it in her mind that I wasn't shit as a man, so her perception of me was never going to change.

I pressed the nurse button while still holding onto Chanel who had tears in her eyes. "Ma, you want that pay medicine now?"

"No, Staten... I want to do it natural," she cried out while still holding onto me.

"You need anything?" the nurse popped her head into the room.

"Yeah, can you show her to the family waiting room?"

"What?" both Chanel and her mother screamed at the same time.

The nurse didn't know what to do. I knew she better had did her job or she was going to get fired tonight. "Yeah, please show her."

"I'm not going nowhere."

"He's the father and he has the right to pick and choose

who he wants in the room." Chanel got a contraction that damn near took her out. She couldn't even protest, so the nurse held the door open for her mother.

"This is what you wanted all along." She pointed her finger at me.

"There you go with those accusations again," I shook my head and watched the nurse close the door. Chanel moved over to the bed and was gripping the end of the bed.

"I needed her here, Staten," she said breathlessly. "She has to be here when I have the baby... she's my mom."

"I'll get her when it's time, but right now she needs to sit her old ass out there."

"Staten!" she screamed. "She's my mother!"

"Shit, I don't care. I'm an adult like she's one. All that shit goes out the window when she trying to paint me out to be some nigga I'm not."

"Well, if the hickie fucking fits."

"How you mad about what is on my body? Matter fact, I'm not doing this right now," I told her and sat down while her ass held onto the bed. Her contractions calmed down, so I got up and helped her into the bed.

"I'm gonna try and get a nap before these shits kick back up again," she told me and rolled on her side. Turning the lights off, I sat in the chair and pulled my phone out to occupy my time. My baby girl was like her daddy; making niggas wait on her. Daddy's girl.

SATIN SUMMER DAVIS came busting in this world through her mama's pussy looking just like her damn mama. Everything about Satin was Chanel. I know people said that your baby came out looking like the person the mother hated her entire pregnancy, but damn ... did Chanel hate her damn self? Either way, my baby girl was so fucking beautiful with her little dimple in her chin and bright brown eyes. They looked hazel to me. The doctor told me that her eye color could change a few times. When I held her, I cried hard as fuck. Tears fell down my face onto her face. Seeing Chanel push her out like a champ without any medicine made me have a new respect for her. She bossed through and didn't complain once. She had a plan and stuck to the shit to get our daughter here.

As much as she got on my nerves this pregnancy, I couldn't thank her enough for carrying and bringing our daughter into this world. She risked her life to bring new life into this world and for that, I was eternally thankful. My mother cried soon as we saw her head pop out. She and Mirror ended up staying in the room since Diana held a damn grudge. Her grudge did nothing except force her to miss her first granddaughter's arrival into the world. She was on FaceTime with Chanel the entire time. I'm not gonna front like I didn't feel bad about the situation. Chanel wanted her mother to be there bad, and she refused to come back to the hospital. It was then when I realized where Chanel got that bratty and baby behavior from. Everyone accused me on spoiling her, that's how she got it. Nah, she had got that shit from her mother and her father did nothing but add to the shit. I can take responsibility and say that I added on and catered to her bratty behavior, but I didn't make her that way. Her parents did all that shit. When her father got on the phone cause the moms was crying, I knew right then and there that I'd knock Chanel out if Satin behaved that way.

How the fuck you make the most important day of your daughter's life about yourself? I didn't understand why the fuck she was so upset when she had been spewing shade and hate the minute I stepped into the room. How long did she think I was going to put up with that shit. Her ass was lucky I put up with it for as long as I did. If it was up to me, she would have been gone when she did that passive aggressive ass greeting.

Still, I tried to be there and support Chanel and allow her mother to be there.

"Let me see her, Staten," Chanel grumbled as she woke from her sleep. "I bet you haven't put her down since I went to sleep," she smiled.

"Nah, I don't ever want to put her down," I kissed Satin's small face and smelled the baby smell that I had grown to love in the twelve hours since she had come into this world

Chanel reached her arms out. "Gimme my baby," she gently took the baby from me and kissed her on the lips. "Mommy prayed so hard for you, Satin," she told her.

"Daddy too." I added.

"Me and Daddy both tried so hard for you too.... That's something you don't need to know either," she giggled.

I sat next to her on the bed. She slowly moved over while wincing. Even though she delivered natural, she was still sore. Satin was eight pounds and had ripped her. A nigga almost passed out when they had to stitch her ass back up down there.

"I know me and you haven't been on the same page lately, Nel. You know how much I love and care for you. We been on different pages, but you know the feelings are the same. I'd do anything for you and now our daughter. Thank you for carrying my seed and delivering a healthy baby. For that, I can't thank you enough."

"Shaliq, don't get me in here crying. You know my hormones are still alive and kicking." She gently nudged me. "I would do it over and over again for you and for her. I'm truly happy."

"Me too." I stared down at both Chanel and Satin.

Omg, look at all that damn hair. She's so beautiful. Tell Chanel congrats, because she did that! Maliah responded to the picture of Satin I had sent her.

Aye. I put work in too.

Barely nigga. She's all Chanel lol

Yeah ight... wyd?

Lying in bed... trying to sleep and can't.

Why?

Not tired. Think I'm bout to hit the block and see what's going on?

It's three in the morning, Maliah

So?

Stay your ass in bed

She didn't reply back. Maliah didn't sleep and she would be in the streets all night. Back then, it didn't bother me. Now that we were fucking, it bothered me that she was trying to head out at this time. Business still continued; I knew this. Yet, I didn't want her out there at this time. The shit was mad weird.

"You should go shower and get some rest. You've been up here since yesterday."

"You trying to say I stink?" I joked.

"A little," she snickered. "My parents are coming up around six and I don't want no issues between you and them.

I understood, so she didn't need to explain anything more. Her parents were everything and like my mother had the opportunity to hold her granddaughter, she wanted her mother to do the same.

"Let me kiss my baby." She handed me Satin and I kissed her on the lips. "Daddy will be back. Don't you grow too much while I'm gone."

"I should have recorded you baby talking to her. Big bad ass Staten baby talking to his daughter," she teased.

"I wish you would," I nudged her and kissed her on the forehead. "I'll be back around lunch. I'm gonna bring some food too, so don't eat."

"K," she said as she unwrapped Satin and kissed her small toes. I didn't want to leave my daughter. Damn, did that make me a dad? I finally got the courage to leave out and headed over to Maliah's crib.

I stood at the door ringing her door bell for what seemed like twenty minutes. She finally came and opened the door. Her hair was all over her head and she had drool on the side of her lips.

"We were just texting not too long ago. The fuck you were doing?" I pushed into the house and went into the kitchen. A nigga was hungry as shit. I was so damn nervous and excited for my baby to be born that my ass wasn't thinking about food. Now that she was here, I was hungrier than a hostage.

"I fell asleep on your dumb ass."

"Dumb? What the fuck I did to you?"

She rolled her eyes. "Staten, I know were messing around and shit, but you can't start treating me like I haven't been running the same streets you have."

I couldn't front, she had a point. She had a job to do and she did the shit well. I couldn't start making her stay home and treating her like she didn't know how to handle herself, cause she did.

"My fault." I walked over to her and towered over her. "You gotta run your shit and I need to respect that."

"Thank you," she replied. "How's everything with Chanel and the baby? How do you feel? I'm so excited for you."

"Good. They both good. My daughter is everything to me, man. She ain't even been here a month and I'm already wanting to switch how the fuck I move and think."

"As you should. My mom said when she had us she would give her life to protect us."

"I bet."

"You're gonna do just fine. I know it."

I bent down and kissed her on the lips. "It's something about you, Maliah. You fucking understand me."

"We're friends before anything. I'll always be here for you. Even with us fucking," she winked.

I pulled her close to me and kissed her on the neck. "Stop leaving hickies on me... I ain't a bitch."

"I can't help it," she moaned.

"Ight. Bet. Go in the room cause you about to take this dick," I demanded.

She smirked and then ran off to the bedroom. I heated up the leftover Spanish food we ordered and then headed to the room. I needed to celebrate with some sex. It was well deserved after the day I had.

11

Justice

The next time you cry it's gonna be in a Rolls Royce – Meek Mill

"How long have these contractions been going on? You're not due for another two months, Justice," she reminded me like I didn't know already.

"A week or so. I've been resting and trying not to do so much around the house," I replied. It was something that I tried not to think about. When it first happened, I should have come to the hospital, but I was scared. I tried to blame it on other things and convince myself that it wasn't contractions.

Kiss saw me bent over the kitchen counter and drove me here. We had been calling Priest for the past few hours and he hadn't answered once. Lately, things around the house had been tensed. He seemed like he didn't want to be there or something. Our usual date nights never happened, and he was gone more and more. I was stressed the fuck out worried about what was going to happen with our relationship. The only thing that brought me some kind of comfort was that I was carrying our baby girl. Feeling her move was what kept me going. I hated that I put her life in jeopardy by not coming to get checked out sooner than later.

"You've had about three contractions since we've been talking," she said while looking at her phone, then the machine.

"Let me get a nurse in here to check you," she told me and left the room.

Kiss sat in the corner with Zamari in her arms, asleep. "Jus, you can't have the baby right now," she sighed. "It's too early." I was seven months pregnant. I couldn't give birth right now.

"Have you tried Ro?"

"Yep. I called him so much my phone is about to die," she replied.

I sighed and tried not to get myself worked up. The nurse and the doctor came back, and she prepared to check me. I winced as she stuck her hand up me. "She's five centimeters dilated," she revealed.

"Oh wowwww!" I screamed out after feeling a huge contraction. That shit felt like a damn lighting strike went through my entire body.

"Contraction? They're getting stronger."

I nodded my head quickly. "Much stronger."

"Okay, we're going to give you some medicine to hopefully stop the contraction. My goal is to keep that baby in there for as long as possible," she told me.

The nurse went to get the medicine as they started to get an IV into me. I sat there and allowed them to do everything they needed. It was important for me to make sure my baby was fine. As much as I hated needles, I was going to sit here and do what they told me to do. I dialed Free's number.

"Hey Jus, what's up?" she answered.

"Free, I might be having this baby and I'm so damn scared,"

I cried. "I can't get in touch with Priest and Kiss is here with the baby."

"What? Oh my god! What hospital are you at?"

"Richmond," I told her.

"I'm on my way now. Call Lib and tell her to come too."

"K." I ended the call and dialed Liberty's number. She didn't answer the first time but answered on the second.

"I'm not in the mood to dis---"

"I'm almost sure I'm going to have your niece and I'm scared."

"Wait, what? You're too early."

"I'm having contractions and I'm dilated," I informed her. "I know we're mad at each other, but can you please come? I need you."

"Without a question. I'm coming right now. Which hospital?"

"Richmond," I told her.

"On my way," she said and ended the call.

Hearing how my sisters dropped everything to come be by my side made me feel good. I loved Kiss for rushing me here and being here, but I knew she was scared like hell. I was scared as fuck too and didn't know what to do or where to turn. Priest needed to answer his damn phone because we both needed him here. I leaned my head back and sent him another text message.

Where are you? I need you. I sent him a message and sighed because now I was worried. Priest always answered the phone. Even if he didn't call back, he would send out a text message. We had been calling and texting since Kiss decided to drive me and he hadn't responded yet. What the hell was going on? I wasn't a fool to believe that nothing could never happen to him. He was in the streets and although things had calmed down, there were still people who disliked him.

"Kiss go home and be with your sisters. Plus, he's probably hungry since we didn't bring his diaper bag."

"I'm not leaving you here. We'll be fine." She was so damn stubborn.

I laughed. "I appreciate you wanting to be here for me, but this is more than you. Baby boy is tired, hungry, and probably needs to be changed. The girls need to get ready for bed soon too. If you want to help me, then go home and hold down the fort until we can get in touch with your brother."

I could tell she wasn't happy, yet she listened and understood what I was saying. "Okay. I'll call you the moment he calls me and please let me know if anything happens... don't forget," she warned and kissed me on the cheek. I kissed Zamari on the head and then she headed out of the room. Whatever the nurse put in my IV made the contractions ease up and I was feeling sleepy, so I closed my eyes and decided to get some rest.

Freedom barged into the room with her big ole belly and a whole lot of demands. She wanted to know what was going on, the plan of action, and who was going to be the doctor for the night. It wasn't a laughing matter, but having my big sister there made me feel so much better. Even with her own baby's health issues, she was here and ready to take on the whole staff if she had to.

"You drove here?"

"No, Ghost is parking the car. He refused to let me leave alone."

I laughed because Ghost would always protect Freedom and their children. "You need to sit down because you have to remember you're pregnant."

"I'm fine. The doctor gave me my induction date next week. We need to worry about keeping your baby in a bit longer."

"Free, please sit down. I don't want you stressing out. Calm down, you haven't sat down once since you came into the room."

"I just ran into Ghost. He was throwing up in the trash outside the hospital... he good?" Liberty entered the room.

"He has some stomach bug. I told him he needed to rest, but he insisted on coming anyway. That man is so hard headed."

"Well, I see why y'all a match made in heaven," Liberty mumbled and came over to hug me. "How are you feeling?"

"Better now. I had so much pressure down there that I could barely walk to Kiss's car."

"Where is she now?"

"I told her to head home to keep an eye on the girls and to tend to the baby."

Liberty sat down. "And where the fuck is Priest?"

It was a question that I wanted to know. "I've been calling him, and he hasn't answered. That's not like him at all."

"I'm gonna go and tell Ghost to call him and see if he can through to him." Free left out the room to find Ghost.

"I'm sorry about our lunch. We shouldn't pry and tell you what to do with your life. I hated when you both did it when I was with Todd. I can understand where you're coming from and why you got some angry," I apologized.

It was true. As much as we wanted to spend time and know what Liberty was doing, we had the habit of prying into her business and trying to tell her how she should live. When both she and Free used to gang up on me, I hated. I hated that they tried to tell me how to live my life like I wasn't a grown woman. Liberty lived her life for her, and who was I to tell her that she was living it wrong? All that mattered was that she was clean and doing what needed to be done when it came to Chance. As far as her relationship with Staten, it wasn't our business. As much as we loved Staten, it was Liberty's choice on who she wanted to be with. I prayed they found their way back to each other in the future. However, if they didn't, I had to support my sister. I never wanted her to feel like no one supported her because that wasn't the case. We supported her so much that we sometimes didn't know when we were overstepping our boundaries.

"He's gonna call. Your doctor is briefing the new doctor too."

"She's leaving already?"

"Has another patient who is currently in labor, so she can't be in two places at once," she informed me. Leave it to Free to find out information about my doctor before me.

She walked over to me and rubbed my stomach. "Baby girl, we want to see you so bad, but we can wait a few more months," she spoke to my stomach.

"Already giving me hell and she's not even here yet." I smiled to lighten the mood. "How are you feeling about your induction date?"

"Wait, you got an induction date?" Liberty blurted.

"Yeah. You would know if you answered the phone or call," Free rolled her eyes.

While I was quick to get over an argument, Free and Liberty could hold a fight for months. Our mother always said it was because they had been fighting since they were in her stomach. I smiled thinking about my mother. We still hadn't spoken, and she was just as bad with holding a grudge like Free. She was in Jamaica with her friends and I didn't want to tell her this news. I'd rather wait until she was back to tell her about me and the baby. In my head, I knew that we would be home tomorrow resting in bed. My baby girl wasn't going to come early, I had faith that she wouldn't.

The doctor rushed into the room with three nurses behind him. He scared all of us with the way he flew into the room. "The machine is on silent, so it doesn't disrupt you, but every-thing comes through to our computers out there. The baby's heart rate has dropped rapidly." He was worried, I could see it all in his face.

"What does that mean?" I panicked as Liberty stood up and grabbed hold of my hand.

"Baby doll, that means we need to put some oxygen on you and let me move you slightly to switch your position, that helps as well," the Spanish nurse came over and put the oxygen mask over my face.

She and the other nurses then moved me slightly while the doctor continue to monitor the baby's heartbeat. "Okay. It's going up again with the oxygen and movement. Did you administer the meds to relax her uterus?" he questioned his nurses.

"Yes," she replied. "Gave it to her about an hour or so ago."

"Okay. We'll keep this on. I want to let you know, if the heartbeat goes down again, we're going to deliver the baby. I can't have the baby in there in distress. I'll call up to the NICU, so they're prepared in case this has to happen. I'm hoping that it doesn't, and the baby is just stressed from you being poked, positioned, and given the medicine, but I want to be prepared."

"Thank you, Doctor," I told him as he looked over the scans from the contractions and then exited out the room.

"This is too much for me," Free sighed and sat down next to Liberty. Liberty took her hand and rubbed her stomach.

"Calm down. I don't need both my sisters popping out babies." She tried to make a joke, but I think we were both in our own world.

I had been flipped and positioned like a damn turkey in a pan with an oxygen mask on and I still hadn't been able to get in contact with Priest. I prayed that he was alright or maybe lost his phone. Everything in me didn't want me to think that he was ignoring me. Things around the house had been tense and I tried to smooth it out. Each time I tried to make it right, he told me that he didn't want to talk about it anymore. I was wrong for bringing up the whole Zoe situation. It was wrong, especially since he had voiced that it hurt him that he had to be

JAHQUEL J.

the one to alter Kiss's life. When we were arguing it just slipped out. By the time I tried to catch myself, I had saw the disappointment and sorrow in his face. Priest was the love of my life. I believed he saved me from a dark place in my life, so I never wanted to be the one to ever hurt him. I wished like hell that we could turn back the hands of time and make this right. We had a baby on the way, we had to make this right her and for us too.

12

Priest

We can be as happy as we want to be, girl. But, we got to make it work – Neyo

"Hmm, you smell so good that I could just taste you all over again," Lavern giggled as she pecked me on the lips.

I pulled her close and sucked on her bottom lip. "I could say the same about you too." I smirked and placed a kiss on her nose.

We had been held up at the Sheraton hotel in Brooklyn since this morning. What started as a simple breakfast date turned into something else. Did I plan to fuck Lavern for hours at a time when I came to meet her for breakfast? Hell nah. I was coming so we could talk and catch up. One thing led to another and I found myself booking us a suite and pulling her dress up on the elevator. The feeling felt so damn good. It was like a rush I never knew that I had. Lavern brought me back to the old Priest when everything was alright. My sister was alive, my nieces were good and all the troubles I had were passing finals. She made me feel like a teen again and it was something I didn't think I was ready to give up. Not to mention, I felt young for once. I didn't feel like I had to be responsible for so many damn people. The weight of the world was on my shoulders all the time and no one checked to see if I was alright. Laying up in a suite in the middle of the day fucking made me feel like I was the man.

"As much as I want to go round for round with you, I need to call and check up on my baby. My purse is in your car. I'll grab something to drink from the café while I'm down there," she told me as she wrapped a robe around her body and grabbed the key card.

"Don't take too long." I bit my bottom lip as I watched her switch out of the bedroom. Moments later, the door closed behind her.

I felt like shit for cheating on Justice while she was pregnant. The shit wasn't supposed to happen, and she didn't deserve this shit. She trusted me after her ex-nigga, and I ended up hurting her too. It was different. As much as I love Justice and wanted to make her my wife, I realized shit moved too fast with us. I desired the type of love that we had and thought I was ready for that next step. I don't know, maybe I am still ready for what we have. Lavern popping back into my life did something to me. I couldn't describe the shit, but I was trying to sort it in my head before I spoke about it to anyone. It sounded crazy as fuck when said out loud, but in my head it made perfect sense. Was it so bad to chase a small piece of my old life? Lavern did that for me. She reminded me of all the good times. When we used to do more fucking than studying, or when she would be in the kitchen with Sandy cooking. All that shit lit my soul of fire. I wanted to feel that again.

"You left your phone in the car. It was ringing when I was grabbing my stuff," Lavern came upstairs and sat her purse on the night table. She handed me the phone and I had so many messages and phone calls that I couldn't pin point who they were all from.

Leaning up in the bed, I took the phone and scrolled through my contacts. I dialed Ghost's number since he was the last person who called. "Yo!" his voice boomed through the phone. He was so loud that you would have thought I had the shit on speakerphone.

"You good? What happened?"

"Nigga, Justice is being prepped for a C-section. The baby's heart rate and Justice's went down, and the doctor wants to take the baby out." He informed me. My heart dropped to the floor. As he filled me in, I scrolled my phone and saw so many messages and text messages from her that it broke my heart. I could tell that she was scared as fuck from the text messages begging me to answer the phone.

"What the fuck? She's too early!" I raised my voice and got up to find my clothes. "What hospital? I'm on my way."

"Richmond. Where the fuck you at and why haven't you answered your phone?"

"I'll fill you in when I get there. Please keep them from delivering that baby, I need to be there," I begged.

"Man, if she gotta go in, then she gotta go. I'll go in with her if you don't make it," he promised me. "Free and Liberty too emotional and she need someone strong to go in with her."

"Tell her that I'm coming and that I love her," I told him.

"Got you. Just hurry the fuck up." He ended the call. I pulled the GPS up on my phone and it was going to take me forty minutes to make it there.

"Wow. That just made it real what we're doing." She walked over to the couch near the window and sat down. "I'm tearing a family apart," she sighed and put her head into her hands.

"Nah, it takes two to tangle. I knew what I was doing was

wrong," I told her as I shoved my feet into my sneakers. "I gotta head to the hospital, so I'll hit you when I know more."

"Drive safe," she walked over to me and kissed me on the neck. "I'm praying everything is alright."

"Me too. Don't leave the suite. Enjoy everything on my tab."

"Don't tell me that," she giggled. "Hurry up and get to that hospital." She encouraged as she pushed me toward the door.

"Later." I said and rushed down the hall. I needed to turn a forty-minute drive into twenty minutes without getting caught by the cops.

When I got into my whip, I pulled up the Waze app on my phone so it could alert me of cops during my drive. I sped out of the underground garage doing seventy miles per hour. If the lord wanted me to see my baby enter this world, he would help me out when it came to traffic and the cops.

They bringing her down now, Ghost sent me a text message and my chest started to beat even faster. Tears were burning my eyes as I gripped the steering wheel. I couldn't miss my daughter being brought into this world. This shit was so fucked up and I was paying for my foul ways. This was my fucking karma for being held up in a hotel fucking Lavern all day. I looked at the time on the GPS and I had saved ten minutes by doing eighty-five in a fifty-speed zone. I just needed to make it to that hospital. If I missed it, I would never forgive myself for what I was doing when Justice needed me the most. She never asked for anything and just wanted me there. We hadn't been seeing eye to eye lately and shit in the house was fucked up because of it. I was being stubborn instead of allowing her to make things right. Instead, I brushed her off because I was hurting. Being the man that killed my nephew's pops is something that I carried all the time. Every time I looked into his eyes, there was guilt that I held. When he got older, Kiss had to be the one to explain that his father was killed.

Then adding that it was his uncle that did it, added a

whole other level of hurt. Zamari wasn't even a year and I was already planning a conversation I knew I would have to have with him when he was older. The thought of breaking his heart after I broke his mother's heart brought tears to my eyes. While I was trying to be happy and start a family with Justice, I couldn't enjoy it. Zoe had done dirt and that was the reason he ended up being killed. However, while I was starting a family with the woman I loved, Kiss was trying to deal and cope with being a single mother alone. She acted like she was fine, yet the truth of the matter was that she wasn't happy. She should have been having a man to help with the responsibilities of raising her son. Yeah, I paid for the financial part and stepped in when I could, but she needed and wanted that boy's father. No amount of money I could offer could give her that.

I pulled up to the hospital parking lot and didn't give a damn that I parked in a handicap parking spot. I rushed up to the labor and delivery floor and that's where I saw Free, Kiss, and Liberty sitting in the waiting area. When Kiss saw me, she jumped up and ran over to me.

"Where the hell have you been? I've been calling you like crazy?" she questioned like she was my fucking mother.

"I was handling business. How long ago did they go down?" With me driving crazy, I had got here in thirty minutes instead of the forty. It still wasn't fast enough, but I was happy that I had made it here.

"Twenty-five minutes ago," she replied.

"Where's the baby and what are you doing here?"

"Love is watching Kiki and Zamari ... Justice called me and told me, and I couldn't sit home waiting around for news. You got some nerve asking questions when you were gone and not answering the phone.... Who were you with?"

"Chill the fuck out, Kiss!" I hollered. She was hounding me like a damn rabid dog or something. I was trying to find something out and she was questioning me about shit that didn't matter right now.

"Both of you need to calm down before security escorts you both out," Free came over to me. "Both Justice and the baby's heart rate went so low that not even oxygen could help. The doctor made the call to deliver the baby early. The NICU nurses and equipment is already in the operating room. Soon as Yasmine is born, she'll be transferred upstairs where they will make sure she's doing alright. More than likely, Justice won't get to see her until tomorrow," Free informed me of everything that I needed to know.

"Do they know why the heart rate is down?"

"Kiss brought her here because she was having contractions. The doctor was able to slow the contractions down, but then the baby's heart rate started to decrease. After he got it stabled, that's when Justice's heart rate started to do the same. It was the best and only choice to save both of their lives."

I put my hand over my face and paced the floor. "Ghost went in there?"

"Yeah, I couldn't do it. I'm already feeling faint," she told me.

I walked her back over to the seat. "Sit down. We don't need anything happening to you too. You good, Lib?"

"Yeah, soon as you tell me where you been?" she sat there with her legs crossed, arms folded and a smug look on her face. "She called, text, and even tried to email you. Why weren't you answering?"

"I had a business meeting that I couldn't miss. My phone was in the car. I didn't think she was having the baby today," I lied.

"She said she had been having pressure and pain down there for at least a week. Justice didn't tell you that?" she fished. I knew Justice probably told them that shit at home hadn't been the best between us.

"You think I would have gone to this meeting? Justice's ass would have been at the hospital soon as she told me about it."

"Right. She told us about how it has been around the house. You don't think that stressed her out? You walking around and giving her the cold shoulder because she made a mistake?" Liberty was right about how I had been treating her. The way I was acting definitely added to her stressing out and stressing the baby out.

"I haven't been myself and shit. It's my fault and I'm feeling that. I don't need you fucking telling me what I did under my own roof. Me and Justice's issues are our own. I get she vents to you and shit, but don't get it twisted, that's my woman and our issues will get handled with the two of us," I told her.

When she was running around here getting high off pixie sticks, I kept my mouth shut and didn't add my two cents into it. She needed to give me that same respect that I had gave her. I sat down and put my head into my hands and said a prayer. I never questioned God once. Not even when he took my sister from me. This is the one time I'm questioning and I'm asking for him to make sure both Justice and our daughter were good. There wasn't a lot I asked for, but this was at the top of wish list I had ever made as a child. I needed them to be alright. God shouldn't punish them because I fucked up. I needed them to be alright. Shit take me if you had to, but don't make my daughter and girl pay for the foul shit I did today.

"SHE'S PERFECT, MAN," Ghost said as he came down the hall dressed in the whole blue hospital attire.

"For real? How is she? How is Justice?" I asked him all my questions at once. Waiting to hear news had been the worst thing I had ever faced. I was a wreck and couldn't close my eyes because I needed to know what was going on with Justice and the baby. Shit, if they had a damn owl in the operating room, they needed to send it with some news. When I saw Ghost walking down the corridor, I jumped to my feet and me him half way.

"She was struggling to breathe, so they took her out and had her in the incubator in under five minutes. The doctors rushed her upstairs. Shit had me scared as shit," Ghost explained. "Justice is stable and being brought to the ICU. They want to monitor here since her heart rate did the opposite while being cut open."

"Seriously? Is she awake and talking?"

"Yeah, she's awake and she's talking. They have her on oxygen. I came to show y'all the picture I was able to snap before they whisked her away."

Liberty, Free and Kiss jumped up to look at his phone. It was a picture of a tiny light skin baby with tubes and tape already on her face. "How much did she weigh?" Free was the first to ask.

"She weighed three pounds, two ounces. Justice decided on Yasmine Heaven Mooney," he informed us.

"Damn...." I cursed myself. "I knew she was going to keep Yasmine, but the Heaven shit is so beautiful."

"They're bringing Justice up to the ICU now, so only two people at a time can come in." he explained to us.

"I'm bout to go—"

"She's still being transported. Give them a few to get her settled. Let me holla at you for a minute," he held onto my shoulder.

"What was this meeting that Priest had to attend? It must have been important if he couldn't bring his phone in, right?" Free stood there with her hand propped on her hip.

Ghost looked at me and then at Free. "What you think I'm about to talk to him about? Business is still business and I don't involve you in that," he covered for me perfectly.

Free's facial expression told me she was satisfied with what he had told her. She wobbled her ass back to her seat and sat down. Ghost took me down the hall near the soda and coffee machines.

"Business meeting? Where the fuck were you?" he demanded to know. I didn't want to tell him right now, but since he was there to hold Justice's hand when I couldn't, he deserved to know.

"Me and Lavern was kicking it."

"Kicking it? Movies or lunch type shit?" I knew he was going to be the one to dig deep into what I was doing with Lavern. He was the main one telling me not to get too deep with her and look where I landed myself?

"We went to breakfast..." I leaned forward and lowered my voice. "We ended up at a hotel fucking the shit out of each other." I whispered.

Ghost walked away and then came back over to me. "Are you fucking crazy?"

"I know, but it's different with Lavern. She reminds me of the good days when everything wasn't so high stressed and shit."

"Nigga, you have a girlfriend and a fucking baby. Why the fuck you chasing some old bitch that used to mean something to you?" he harshly whispered.

"Cause it felt fucking good to do something for me for once. I'm always doing what everyone wants me to do and never got shit to myself. Lavern was something I had to myself. She knew the girls, but in the end, she was mine... I don't know it makes sense in my head," I gave up trying to explain shit to him.

"I got fucking cancer and would kill to have the clean bill of health that you have to spend with my family. My health could end me tomorrow, but you have tomorrow and you're fucking what you have up for a bitch you used to fuck back in the day?" he roared.

"Cancer?" we heard Free's voice break from behind him.

"What do you mean by cancer, Gyson?" her voice shook as she walked closer to him.

"They said we can go back and see Jus..." Liberty's voice trailed off. "What happened that quick?" she saw her twin's face as her hands shook.

I dipped to head to see Justice. This wasn't a conversation I wanted to be a part of. Ghost had his reasons for keeping this away from Free, so I didn't fault him. All the stress was not good for her or the baby. Liberty was right behind me as I zoomed down the hall to the elevators that took us up to the ICU. I wanted to see my baby girl bad as shit, but I wanted to make sure that Justice was alright. When I entered the room, she had an oxygen mask over her face and her eyes were closed. I walked over and touched her hands. Her eyes fluttered open and she stared at me with a smile, then the smile faded. The look of love turned to a look of hate as she snatched her hand back.

"Baby, what's wrong?" I questioned as I tried to grab her hand back. "You good? Need me to call the nurse in?"

She removed the oxygen mask off her face. "That's a nice shade of lipstick on the side of your neck," her voice was low and raspy.

Liberty walked over to me and observed. "How did I miss that? That must have been an intense meeting today, huh?" she chuckled and walked on the opposite side of Justice.

"Where were you, Ro? Don't lie to me?" she insisted on knowing.

"Ma right now isn't the right time. We'll talk about it. We need to focus on you and the baby," I tried to convince her. It was true though. We needed to focus on the baby, not where I was at.

"Tell me," she demanded.

"Justice come on. We don't need to talk about this right

now." How the fuck didn't I notice the lipstick that Lavern had left on me?

"If you can't be honest with me, leave my r—"

"I was with Lavern," I blurted. She wasn't going to stop asking until I was honest with her. The tears that fell down her cheeks and the look that was on her face hurt me. In that moment with Lavern, everything felt so right. Now looking at the hurt I caused Justice made me feel like shit.

"I'm gonna go in the hall and let you both talk. What hurts the most is that she trusted you when she had given up on trusting men. It's fucked up, Priest, real fucked up," Liberty said as she left the room.

Justice's hands were shaking as she tried to wipe away all the tears. "I asked you if she was gonna be a problem and you told me no," she sobbed. "I told you my fears and you told me not to worry. Did you sleep with her?" she questioned.

I looked down at my feet. "Yeah."

"Get the fuck out of my room. I was worried sick about you and trying to hold this baby inside me, while you were fucking another bitch! Fucking another bitch was worth missing your daughter's birth!" she screamed and tossed the water bottle that was next to her. The machine next to her was going crazy. The nurse came into the room to see what the commotion was about.

"You need to calm down. Your heart rate is dangerously high," she told her and tried to put the mask back over her face.

"Get the fuck out now!!!!" she screamed again.

"Sir, please leave." The nurse told me, and I walked out the room. I felt like shit for what I had caused. The nurses and doctor ran into the room when I left out. My heart felt like it had been shot a million times and then left on the highway. Why the fuck did I do this?

13

Liberty

Shame on me for changing... no, no, shame on you for staying the same – Jhene Aiko

A Few Weeks Later...

"Fucking cancer. He lied to me about cancer," Free complained as she pumped breast milk for the baby.

She had Samoor Jyson Davis a few weeks ago and he was still in the NICU. I had been spilt between both of my sisters. Justice had been discharged, but Yasmine had to remain in the hospital for a few months. She had spent all her time there or at my condo. Samoor and Yasmine were at different hospitals, so I had to drive from one to the next to check on my niece and nephew. Samoor had to have surgery soon as he was pulled out of Freedom. It was hard on all of us because we were so worried about him. He pulled through surgery and was doing well enough to go home this week. Free had dark circles around her eyes, her hair hadn't been combed and I could tell she hadn't had a shower in a few days. Her days revolved around Samoor and trying to be there for Ghost. Since we all found out about him having cancer, our entire world had been rocked.

How and why did he hide this from us? We needed to be there for him through this time. As strong as Ghost was, I could tell he was scared. Cancer wasn't something light and knowing that he was in stage two was what made it even scarier. To take the load off my sister, I made sure to come and get the kids ready for school and help as much as I could. She had a lot on her plate, and I didn't want her having a mental breakdown because she had all of this on her mind. I had even taken some personal time off from work to be there for both Justice and Freedom. When it rained, it fucking poured. My family was going through a lot and it was crazy as fuck. I would sit home at night and get high, so I didn't have to think about the shit. There was no reason to complain because if I was stressed then I could only imagine how both my sisters were feeling. It would be selfish of me to complain about my stress and not take theirs into consideration as well.

"You don't need to be focused on the fact that he didn't tell you. He had a good reason for not telling you. It doesn't mean it was right, but he had good reason," I replied.

"I don't care if I couldn't be stressed. Something like that you tell your partner. I feel so empty and hurt," she sniffled. Free had been so emotional. It was the hormones and the fact that she happened to be going through a lot right now in her life. "I don't know what me and the kids would do without him," she sniffled.

"Don't think like that. He's going to fight this and that's all that matters," I tried to be positive. On the inside I was freaking out and worried about what would happen.

"Liberty, he took me to his lawyer and had me sign

guardianship papers for Rain. If something happened to him, he wanted to be sure that I raised her with the kids." She wiped tears away as she took her breast off the pump.

"He's being careful and getting his ducks in the row. Somebody shooting him could kill him before cancer.... God forbids. Stop thinking so negative, Free. After what happened to Summer, I don't blame him for being safe and getting things handled."

She stood up and went to put the bottled milk into the cooler bag before going to the closet to switch her clothes. "I need to head to the hospital to bring this milk, and then I have to go sit with Ghost."

"Let me take it," I offered. "I've been up there nearly every day. I'll take the milk and then you go sit with Ghost. That way you both can come up to see Samoor when he's done," I suggested.

She pondered for a second and then agreed. "Okay. Tell his nurses that I'll be up." She told me as I got up.

"Do me a favor and take a shower before going to sit with Ghost. You're smelling a little ripe."

She rolled her eyes. "Whatever."

I grabbed the milk bag and headed downstairs. Free had been going through so much so I wanted to make things easier on her. When Justice asked to come move in with me, I let her come stay with me because I knew what she was going through with she and Priest. Priest called her every day and tried to talk to her when she was up visiting Yasmine. My nigga was stupid to fuck something up with Justice. She was everything that a man could ever want, and he fucked that up for a bitch that he used to fuck with back in the day. How stupid could you be?

Thinking about you, I smiled at the message from Ty. He had been so sweet during this time. We hadn't seen each other in weeks and he still called every day and made an effort. It was getting harder to try and end things because I was actually growing to like him. It was different with him. Maybe it was because he didn't know my secret, so that's probably why he didn't treat me any different.

I closed my truck door and pulled my phone out. *I was just thinking about you too. Can't wait to see you soon.*

Looking forward to it, he replied.

I headed to the hospital with a smile on my face because of Ty. All it took was one text to lift my spirits up and make me feel so much better. With all that had been going on in my life, it was nice to have a small piece of sunshine to myself. Both Justice and Free needed me and I had to be there for them. I dialed Justice to see if she needed me to pick her up and drop her to the hospital.

"Hey," she answered. Justice always sounded so up and now she sounded dry when you spoke to her. The only time she had somewhat of a smile was when she was spending time with Yasmine.

"You need a ride to go and see Yasmine?"

"No, I'm gonna catch an Uber," she yawned. "I've been trying to get myself up and dressed for the past hour," she sighed.

"Yasmine isn't going to be mad if you took a day to get some rest. Justice, I see you up every morning and you're tired as hell," I tried to convince her. "I'll even go and check on her for you," I offered.

"Priest is going up there right now so I'm trying to wait until he leaves before going up there."

"When are you both going to sit down and talk? I'm not forcing you or anything, just want to know. It's been weeks since you have spoken a word to him."

"I'm not going to sit down and talk to him. For what? He wanted to go and chase his old bitch, let him talk to her," she snapped.

"Sorry. Didn't want to piss you off."

"Oh, you didn't piss me off. I'm just telling you that I'm not in the right space to talk to him. I'm just pissed that I allowed myself to fall for another man that hurt me and didn't give a fuck," she vented.

"I hear you. Get some rest and I'll see you later when I go visit Yasmine. Call me when you head up there, okay?"

"Okay. Oh, and thanks for letting me stay here, Lib."

"You're my baby sister. I have a place and you needed a place, no questions asked," I replied. Even though I loved having my own space, I didn't mind sharing my apartment with my sister. She didn't want to be in Priest's house anymore and needed to leave. She could have gone to Free's house, but she said she knew they were going through so much so she didn't want to be an added burden.

"Thanks Liberty," she replied.

"Talk to you in a little bit," I replied and ended the call.

I arrived at the hospital and headed to the NICU. After scrubbing in and handing the nurses the milk, I sat down and stuck my hand into the incubator to touch Samoor. He had been taken off the breathing machines and the next step was to see how he was going to do outside the incubator for a long period of time. I touched his small hand and smiled. Samoor was six pounds when he was born and now, he was a little over seven pounds. Free made sure to give him only breast milk. The woman was like a cow. She pumped so much and then brought it up to the hospital so they could feed him when she wasn't here to feed him. Samoor was a greedy little thing too. Looking at my nephew made me feel so warm on the inside. He reminded me so much of Samaj. It was crazy how his little facial expressions brought me back to when Samaj was his age. Ghost's genes were strong as shit.

"Is mama coming up today, or just you?" the nurse who took care of Samoor asked, as she looked over and added things to his charts.

"She and Gyson will be up here later on. They had something to handle before coming here," I replied.

"Good. He looks around and it's like he's looking for his mama or something," she chuckled. "His feeding is now; you want to feed him?"

I nodded my head yes. When I came, he was usually fed and already sleeping. "I would love to."

She gently handed me a receiving blanket to put over my shoulder and then opened his incubator to take him out. He had the heart and pulse monitor attached to his foot so you couldn't move too far from the incubator.

"I'm going to go get the other babies ready for feeding. When you're done, you can just burp him and then put him back inside whenever you're ready," she informed me.

"Okay, thank you again."

"No problem." She gently touched my shoulders and went to get the other babies ready for feeding.

"Samoor, you're so lucky. Your parents and siblings love you so much. They can't wait until you come home so they can spoil you," I softly spoke to him. "Auntie loves you too. I'll try to come around more and spend time with you and your siblings more often. Your mommy better not have no more babies either," I giggled.

He sucked down the bottle and did a small smile. "Ah, you're smiling at me or playing with your big sister up there. Make sure you tell her that we miss and love her." I kissed him on the forehead as he finished the rest of his bottle. It felt good being off from work and spending time in the NICU with Samoor. The lights were low, it was quiet and there was soft music playing. Shit, this was better than a damn spa if you asked me. I continued to hold and cuddle him while feeding him.

"Oh, I didn't know you were up here," Staten's voice caused me to look up. He was dressed in a pair of sweats that showed that print, white t-shirt, jean jacket, and a fresh pair of Nikes.

I finished burping Samoor and placed him gently in the incubator. "I came to bring the milk for Free. She's going to sit with Ghost at chemo," I explained.

"Yeah, he told me. I came to see how little dude was doing," he replied. "I'll let you have your time and come back." He turned and walked toward the door.

"Um, Staten, can we talk?" I had been putting off talking to Staten for too long.

My heart couldn't lie like I didn't miss him. He was someone who I spent a lot of time with, opened up to, and trusted. Going from talking to him every day to not talking at all hurt me slightly. A few times I was going to call him, then I remembered he switched his number. With me and Ty hanging out, it was easy to distract myself from the breakup between me and Staten. Every so often he crossed my mind and I wondered what he was doing. The truth of the matter was that I missed him, and I couldn't act like I didn't. Plus, the way I ended things; he didn't deserve that. Especially when all he was trying to do was love me and I was fighting him on it.

"Yeah," he said and left the NICU. I followed out behind him and we headed near the bathrooms. "What's good?"

"Nothing. I just wanted to talk. We haven't spoken in so long and I miss you," I admitted. My ass was being so damn transparent right now.

"What you think happens when you break up with someone?" he shot back. It was different getting the cold side of him. Staten had never been that way with me and witnessing how cold he could be made me feel a type of way.

"I know, but I thought that we would still hang out like we used to." I was hopeful that even though we were ending our relationship that we would continue with our friendship.

I leaned back on the wall and waited for him to respond.

"Liberty, how the fuck you thought that would happen? I'm in love with you. Did you think I would be able to be around you and be fine?"

"I mean... I just don't want things to be weird between us. I miss you, Staten... My fear is that you'll move on and find someone who deserves a man like you."

He chuckled and wiped his hand over his face. "Why the fuck is that your fear? I fucking deserve to be loved too, Lib. The sun doesn't fucking rise and set on only you," he raised his voice and then got it under control.

A tear slid down my cheek. "Are you messing with someone else?"

"It doesn't matter. You happy, right? You got what you wanted so that's all that matters."

"No, I'm not. I'm missing you and too stubborn to tell you." I walked over to him and held the side of his face. He looked away but stayed there so I could touch his face. Reaching up, I kissed him on the lips. "I missed feeling you inside of me too."

Staten shoved me into the family bathroom and locked the door behind him. He pulled my dress up and leaned on the counter. Pulling his sweats down, he shoved his dick inside me as I moaned out and held onto his shoulders. I kissed him on the lips, and he didn't kiss me back. Instead, he pulled me closer to him and shoved more of himself inside of me. I tossed my head back and enjoyed feeling him inside of me. It had been too long and feeling him inside of me felt like everything was perfect again. I regretted ending things with Staten. Now that I had seen him, I wanted him now more than everything.

"Harder, baby," I moaned, and he did as I requested. He held onto my ass cheeks and gripped the shit out of it as we fucked on the edge of the sink. I wrapped my legs around him and kissed him on the neck and tried to be more affectionate. I felt nothing back in return. He gripped my hair, pulled my head back, and dug deeper and deeper.

"I'm bout to nut," he called out and I was grinding my hips against him about to do the same thing. "Shitttttt," he groaned and went stiff.

"Oh goodness, I've missed you," I still sat on the edge of the sink as he pulled his pants up. "What you doing later?" I questioned. He had to stop by and break me off with some more because this wasn't going to hold me over.

He held his hand up and answered his phone. "What's good, ma? Nah, I'm heading to you now," he smirked as he spoke on the phone. "Hold on really quick." He pulled the phone from his ear. "I'll holla at you, ight?" he told me and walked out of the door.

I stood there on the edge of the sink with my pants down feeling so fucking low. How could he pick up the phone and speak to another bitch in my face? Then to leave me here like some whore he fucked in the bathroom after knowing for ten minutes. My feelings were so fucking hurt. Tears fell down my face as I pulled my dress down and stared into the mirror. Did he not find me attractive anymore? Was I not enough? Who was the woman on the phone? All these questions were going through my head and causing me to feel sick. I ended things with him and now he wanted nothing to do with me. Staten used to eat out the palm of my hands and now he didn't even want to be bothered. I had heard about Chanel having their daughter and he didn't bother to tell me. We used to tell each other everything and now I felt like I wasn't a part of his life anymore. It hurt so bad that I had to sit in the bathroom for a few minutes longer to pull myself together. At this moment, I was feeling like I had ruined what we had, and I wouldn't be able to get it back, no matter how hard I tried.

14

Maliah

Looking perfect, surrounded by artificial, you're the closest thing to real I see – Neyo

I knew this would happen. I just knew that I would end up caught up like this. My life would be going perfect and this would happen, these were thoughts that were going through my head as I paced my bathroom waiting for the results of the pregnancy test. I hadn't been feeling sick or anything, but my period was late. My period was clockwork and was always on time. Me and Mariah were on the same cycle. When she called me complaining about cramps like she did every month, I knew I was in trouble. My period always started before hers and mine was nowhere in sight a week later. Not even a small period cramp to give me the warning to put a pad on. Me and Staten had been having sex and haven't been using protection. I didn't think protection was a thought on either of our minds. Soon as we saw each other, it was on and then we would lay in bed, floor, or counter too tired to move. I wanted to slap myself for withholding from sex for so damn long. I couldn't get enough. Staten was teaching me how to become more comfortable with my body and sex. When we first started, I was so stiff and allowed him to do all the work.

Staten was different than the Staten I worked with. That man made me feel so fucking beautiful. He made me feel like I could pick the world up and run a 5K with it. It felt nice to have someone amp me up when I needed it. He turned me from wanting to be alone all the time, to wanting to spend time with him. Shaliq Davis was amazing and I was falling for him more and more. Even with him spending most of his time with Chanel and their daughter, I didn't mind. I knew his daughter came first and I respected that. My vibe wasn't to harass him or make him feel like he had to choose who he had to spend his time with. I was fine with him spending time with his daughter and then giving me the time when he wasn't busy. I understood he was busy and was happy with whatever time that he wanted to give me.

"What is the damn emergency?" Mariah walked into the bathroom.

I had called her to come over because it was about time for me to tell her about me and Staten. We were twins and we shared everything with each other. However, keeping this secret from her had felt nice. It was something for me and I didn't have to hear her judging me about what she thought. Mariah had been open about how she felt about my feelings that I had for Staten. I didn't want to hear what she would think about it when I told her that I lost my virginity to him.

"I think I'm pregnant," I blurted as I continued to pace the bathroom. My eyes went to the edge of the counter that the test was sitting on. I refused to look at the test because I felt that I might faint.

"Huh? By who? You have you been fucking and why you haven't told me about it?" she questioned.

"Staten took my virginity," I revealed, and she sat down on the toilet. "What are you talking about?"

"When I took the trip to Belize, he took my virginity and we've been fucking ever since." I sighed and leaned on the bathroom counter.

"And you didn't think to tell me? Mom is going to kill you."

"Mom doesn't need to find out. Did you tell her about Trac right away?" I raised my eyebrow and looked at her. "Don't judge me."

"I'm not. All I'm just saying is why didn't you tell me? Staten has a daughter now and you think he just fell out of love with Liberty over night?"

"He and Liberty are broken up and I know about he and Chanel's baby. I'm grown like you are, Mariah. I know how to handle myself."

"Staten is in his thirties. He's a grown man, too much man for you to handle." She had the nerve to say.

"Too much for me to handle? Just because you lost your virginity first doesn't mean that you're more experienced than me."

I hated when she acted like she knew more than me. Maybe I didn't know how to handle a grown man like Staten, but I could learn. Not every woman learned how to be the perfect woman for a man overnight. Plus, I wasn't trying to be perfect for Staten. I was just trying to be me and wanting him to love me for me.

"What does the test say?" she sucked her teeth and went to the sink. "You want to be so grown but didn't use protection," she snapped as she picked up the test.

"What does it say?"

"You're with child," she gasped. "I can't believe you got pregnant before me," she sat the stick back down on the counter. "Are you going to tell mommy?"

"Who says that I'm even keeping the baby?"

"Are you gonna tell Staten?"

I shrugged because I really didn't know. How could I tell him this? He literally just had a baby not too long ago. Would he be excited, worried, or upset? These were all things I worried about. I didn't want to ruin what we had.

"How often do you both spend time together?" Mariah questioned.

"Whenever he's not running around, spending time with his daughter and being there for his brother. I'm not pressed to spend time because I know he has things to handle and I do too."

"You gotta let him go, Maliah. It's not fair to you, sis. You're settling for a piece of a man. Liberty is that man's heart and while he's spending time and fucking you, he's thinking about her."

I was so aggravated that she had to add her two cents into this. When she was hell over heels for Trac, I never judged her. Instead, I covered for her and supported her. Why was it so hard for her to do the same for me?

"I've supported you when mommy didn't. You loved Trac and I rode for you because I knew how much he meant to you. It seems like shit only works one way when it comes to us, huh?" I walked out of the bathroom and headed downstairs.

I damn near jumped out of my skin when I saw my mother sitting on my couch. She had a cup of tea and her legs crossed. Her foot dangled with her infamous black timberlands on her feet. I slowly walked down the six remaining stairs and walked into the living room.

"How do you have a conversation and then walk..." Mariah's voice trailed off as she got down the rest of the stairs. "What are you doing here, ma?" she questioned.

"I can't come and spend time with one of my daughters?" she shot back and took a sip of her tea. It was piping hot too, so she had been here for a little while. Did she hear our conversation? I prayed she didn't hear anything about what we were talking about.

"You can but knocking or letting us know you were here would have been nice too." I made sure to add. How the hell did she get in? I made sure not to give my parents a key to my place. I wanted privacy and didn't need them popping over whenever they felt like it. Although, my dad would be the one to pop over before my mother would.

"I like my way." She shrugged and continued to drink her tea.

"Let me go and grab my bag," Mariah said and headed back up the stairs. She came jogging back down. "I hid the test," she whispered in my ear.

"See you later," I told her as she headed out the door quickly. Mariah didn't feel like hearing my mother question her about Trac and what she was doing now that she stepped away from the streets.

I sat down on the couch across from her after Mariah left and crossed my legs. The positive pregnancy test upstairs was still on my mind as I sat across from my mother. A baby? I couldn't be someone's mother. It wasn't that I couldn't take care of a child because I had enough money to hire the help I would need. What scared me was that I didn't think I was ready to become a mother.

"You seem distracted," my mom commented.

"Work and trying to get sleep has been a struggle," I lied. Work and sleep were the easiest things in my life right now.

"It was a time when me and your father weren't together. You girls were young, and we couldn't figure things out, so we decided to separate for a while," she revealed.

"For real? I never knew," I lied. Mariah had told me when I

was over her house a while back. Still, I wouldn't tell my mother that I knew.

"I'm surprised your big mouth sister didn't tell you." She lightly chuckled. "I met a man. Fell in love with that man. His name was Rage," she smiled to herself as she reminisced.

"You fell in love with another man? So how did you and daddy find yourself back with each other?"

"I fell hard. I even considered having a life with him. Your father wasn't even a thought whenever I was around him," she sighed.

"So, why didn't you choose him?" I wondered. She had never spoke any of this to me before. To me, my parents were in love and she was his first love. To hear that there was someone else made me wonder if what Mariah told me was really true.

"Sometimes you have to make hard decisions to keep your family together and avoid future issues." She sat her tea cup down on the coaster. "Like the one you need to make about you and Staten." She looked me square in the face.

I was so careful and hadn't told anyone about us fucking around. How did she find out about us? No one knew about Belize and what was going on between us. I had just told Mariah so I knew she couldn't have told her.

"How did you know?"

"Did you really think I wouldn't find out? I'm Messiah Garibaldi. The things that you and your sisters got past me were things I allowed. This? I can't allow. Staten is like family and runs his ship well, so I refuse to have to choose. End it," she demanded.

"How are you going to tell me to end it? Did you ever consider that we might have feelings for each other?"

"I don't care what you feel. End it, Maliah. This can end bad and I don't think you want that."

"You and the Davis' go back years, you wouldn't go against them. Especially for this," I challenged her.

"Try me," she smirked. "Ghost is like a brother to me. Staten is too. You don't cross lines and the both of them know that. I'll handle him personally, Maliah. Try me."

My heart was racing. "We can sit down and talk about this," I tried to convince her there were other ways.

"I trusted him to take my baby girl to Belize and he comes back fucking her. I'm trying hard not to handle it my way. I'm giving you a chance to fix this to avoid me stepping in," she told me.

"I'm not a fucking baby, mami! I'm a grown woman with needs and not the ones that the streets give me. Why can't I be happy?" I screamed.

Still, cool as a cucumber, she sat there unfazed by my tantrum. "You can. Not with Staten," she replied, not caring that I wanted to be with him.

"I'm pregnant and I'm keeping it." Right then and there I decided that I was going to keep my baby.

Very rarely have I ever saw my mother so stunned that it showed on her face. She stood there shocked as she stared at me. "Lies. I refuse to believe it."

"I swear on papa that I'm pregnant," I put it on my grandfather. "I'm keeping my child, so I don't want to hear anything that you have to say."

"You dye your hair this loud ass blonde, fuck Staten who is like family, and bring a bastard baby into this family?"

"According to daddy, we were bastards too."

"Do as I say, not as I do!" she raised her voice. "You will get rid of that baby and end things with Staten. Do it, or I'll handle it my way." She told me as she stood to her feet. I watched as she shook her head and headed to the door. "You heard me. It's final." Were her last words as she left out the door, letting it slam behind her.

I laid on the couch so confused on what to do. In my heart, I knew my mother wouldn't do anything to Staten. I think she wanted to scare me into ending things and getting an abortion. Staten and Ghost were so close with us that she considered them family. My mother was loyal. Maybe too loyal to a default, so I knew she would never bring harm to Staten, even if she didn't agree with the decision he made to have sex with me.

With everything that happened earlier, I was excited when Staten came knocking on my door. It had been a few days since I saw him, and I was excited to hug and be around him. My Decision was still torn if I wanted to tell him about the pregnancy. He had a lot on his plate, and I didn't want to add anymore by laying this on him right now. I was even going to keep quiet about the argument I had with my mother. When it came to family, she was all bark and no bite. She was trying to use her mind tricks to see if I would bite. Just like Mariah, I was standing my ground. She had given Trac the same warning and he was still messing with Mariah, so I wasn't worried about her and Staten didn't need to worry about that either.

"What you been up to, lil bit?" he reached down and kissed me soon as I opened the door. I loved when he called me that. It was because I was so much shorter than him. I was only 5'5".

"Sitting here trying to figure out what I'm gonna do. I'm tired, but then I don't want to sleep," I sighed and went into the kitchen. "Hungry?"

"Nah, I ate over at Chanel's crib. Satin's ass got me good when I changed her diaper," he laughed.

"Awe, how is she doing?"

"Good. Still looking like her mother," he laughed. "I'm waiting for a little piece of me to come through or something."

"She's still young so it will come in. Babies change a million times before they look like who they're supposed to look like," I assured him.

He walked upstairs and I followed behind him. I climbed in bed as he sat on the bench in front of the bed and took his sneakers off. "I fucked Liberty the other day. When you called me and we met up for lunch in Jersey, I had just finish fucking her when you called me to ask where I was."

I dropped my head because I had a feeling. His entire attitude was different. It wasn't like he treated me any different. He just seemed distant and distracted with something. "What does that mean?"

"Nothing. I just fucked her. We're not back together or shit like that."

I crawled to the bottom of the bed and put my arms around him. "How do I know that you won't end up back with her and then it's fuck me?" I wondered out loud.

He pulled my arms tighter around his neck and kissed my hands. "What we doing is nice. It's good. I'm feeling the shit out of you, Maliah. I'm not worried about Liberty. She chose what she wanted and just because we fucked doesn't mean I'm about to be back to kissing her ass," he told me. "You hear me?"

"Yeah, I hear you." I sat back on the bed and watched him undress. He went into the bottom drawer where he kept some shirts and pants and grabbed a pair of shorts and shirt. He paused for a second then turned around with the pregnancy test in his hand. A bitch wanted to fucking faint. Mariah could have put that damn test any damn where and she decided to put it in the drawer that he kept a few things in?

"What's this?"

"I'm pregnant." I started to lie, then I thought about how I hated being lied to and decided to keep it honest with him.

"You serious?"

"Yeah. I've never been on the pill or anything because you know..." I allowed my voice to trail off. What more could I say? "I want to keep the baby too." I decided to lay it all out on the table.

"Then we keeping the baby. Bet." He walked over to the bed and sat beside me.

"You're not mad?"

"Why? Only a fuck nigga would be mad. I know I was running in you without a hat on, so why would I be mad?" he pulled me close to him. "I'm not worried about me; I'm worried about you. I'm in my thirties and I'm ready for kids and all that shit, but you're still young. Is that something you want for yourself right now?"

"I didn't see myself having children. Now that I found out, it's all I keep thinking about. I want to be a mother and raise this baby. I don't think I have it in me to abort the baby."

"Then you shouldn't have to. We both getting to the bag, our baby will be straight," he smirked. "On a serious note, your parents. We gotta be grown ass adults and sit down and tell them." He stood up and walked to the bathroom.

"Uh huh." I nodded and thought about the conversation between me and my mother. A meeting with my father was well needed. He was the only one who could calm my mother down and make her think correctly. He was the one who stepped in for Mariah when my mother wanted to end Trac.

Daddy, we need to talk, I sent a quick text message.

I get in tomorrow from England, come by the house and we'll talk, he replied back almost instantly.

Can you just come by my house? I need to speak to you privately

Got you. I laid back on the bed and closed my eyes. Before I knew it, I was fast asleep.

"Nooooo! Mariah! Watch out!" I screamed out and tossed punches and anything that I could throw.

"Maliah, the hell? Maliah!" I heard Staten's voice and stirred from my sleep. He was leaned up in the bed looking at me crazy. "You good? What the hell was that about?"

"I have night terrors sometimes. Me and Mariah both get them," I admitted. It was the reason that I barely slept. The dirt I did always caught up with my ass in my sleep. It was always the same dream. A nigga that me and Mariah had killed, had come back, and killed Mariah while I watched. The shit caused me to wake up in cold sweats almost daily.

Staten pulled me in his arms and kissed me. "Chill. Calm down and breathe. You gotta start talking about that shit and not bottling that shit up."

"To who? I can't go and talk to a therapist about this."

"Me. Talk to me about it," he said.

I yawned and climbed out of the bed. The bar in my bedroom had water so I grabbed a water out of the mini fridge. "Yeah, maybe one day. Go to bed." I laughed and climbed back in bed. He pulled me into his arms and kissed me on the lips.

"Don't start tripping again," he warned.

"Shut up, stupid," I giggled and snuggled in his chest and fell back asleep.

WE WERE both so tired that we slept the entire morning. All we did was get up to eat, watch a little TV and then went back to sleep. Staten checked in on his daughter and I checked in with my father to see what time he was due to fly in. He never replied when he traveled, so I knew he would show up whenever he got back. I laid across the bed on my stomach watching a John Gotti documentary while Staten rubbed on my booty and watched the sports highlights. We could be in the same room, in our own worlds and have the best time. This felt so good and we didn't have to do much. No fancy restaurants, trying too hard or dressing up. Just us, lying in our underwear enjoying things that we loved. I was surprised that he took me revealing the pregnancy the way he did. I thought he would be upset and ask me to get rid of the baby. Hearing how he stepped up and was down with whatever I wanted made me love him that much more. He cared more about me and my life than he did about his own. It was rare that men thought about someone other than themselves, especially in a situation like this. I continued to watch the documentary unbothered.

"Damn, they almost had it," he commented on the highlights he was watching. "The damn Knicks be making me feel ashamed."

"Leave the Knicks alone," I laughed.

"You the only damn fan. I can get floor seats for five dollars," he joked.

"Nah, what you not about to do is play with the Knicks like that.... Put some respect on their name."

"Yeah, soon as they make it to the finals," he slapped my ass and I giggled. Leaving the iPad, I got on my knees and jumped on him and we play fought on the bed. "Why you fronting like that team not trash?"

"They still my team though," I defended them.

He slapped my ass again and as I straddled him; his phone rang. He hit the green button and the speaker button. "What's good, Priest?" he spoke as he continued to fuck with me.

"Liberty is being rushed to the hospital, she overdosed." All the hair on my arms stood up as Staten tossed me on the left side of the bed.

"What the fuck? She's using again? he barked. "How you know?" he got up and tried to locate some clothes to put on.

"Free just called. Justice came home to grab some things to bring for Yasmine and found her like that. Justice is really fucked up right now."

"Shiiiiitttttt! I should have seen that shit!" he yelled. "What hospital?"

"Staten Island Hospital," he replied.

"I'm on way right now." He ended the call and grabbed his sneakers. "I gotta go."

"Can I drive you? You're freaking out and I don't want you getting in an accident," I asked. His hands were shaking, and he was moving so damn fast he forgot to put a shirt on.

"Yeah, yeah, hurry and get dressed."

I tossed on a maxi dress, jacket, and a pair of Balenciaga sneakers and was heading out the door in under ten minutes. My keys were in my hand as I left the house and locked the door behind us. Soon as I turned around, I saw my mother standing there with her gun pointed at Staten. Staten was so distracted he didn't know she was about to end him.

"Mamiiiiii, No!!" I screamed.

POW! POW! POW!

"Yoo, Messiah what the fuck did you just do?"

To Be Continued

Let me know what you guys think. Sound off in the reviews. Oh, and if you put "It moved slow. Blah, blah, blah." I put in the beginning not to read if you felt that way. Tsk, Tsk hard head makes a soft....lol! Love you, anyway!